1026

LA FEMME NIKITA X-POSED

TED EDWARDS

LA FEMME NIKITA X-POSED

The Unauthorized Biography
of Peta Wilson
and Her On-Screen Character

PRIMA PUBLISHING

This book was not approved, licensed, or endorsed by Peta Wilson or any entity involved in creating or producing *La Femme Nikita*.™

PRIMA PUBLISHING and colophon are registered trademarks of Prima Communications, Inc.

"Idiot's Guide to Section One" used here with permission of author.

Library of Congress Cataloging-in-Publication Data

Edwards, Ted.
    La femme nikita x-posed : the unauthorized biography of Peta Wilson and her on-screen character / Ted Edwards.
        p.   cm.
    Includes index.
    ISBN 0-7615-1454-6
    1. Femme Nikita (Television program)   2. Femme Nikita (Motion picture) I. Title.
    PN1992.77.F395E38   1998
    791.45'72—dc21
                                                                98-25960
                                                                CIP

98 99 00 01 02 DD 10 9 8 7 6 5 4 3 2 1
Printed in the United States of America

```
How to Order
```
Single copies may be ordered from Prima Publishing, P.O. Box 1260BK, Rocklin, CA 95677; telephone (916) 632-4400. Quantity discounts are also available. On your letterhead, include information concerning the intended use of the books and the number of books you wish to purchase.

Visit us online at http://www.primapublishing.com

CONTENTS

CONTENTS

ACKNOWLEDGMENTS

For making this book a reality, I'd like to thank the following people: director John Badham, James Van Hise for his work on the encyclopedia, Terri Malinski for the "Idiot's Guide to Section One," the good folks at *RetroVision* magazine (check out their Web site at www.retrovisionmag.com), and the all-encompassing Internet, which has turned research into a pleasurable experience.

LA INTRODUCTION NIKITA

Luc Besson's *Nikita* was an effective action thriller, and this is coming from one of those nimrods who can't handle subtitles.

John Badham's *Point of No Return* was a fairly pointless, oftentimes shot-by-shot remake of Besson's work that didn't bring anything new to the table.

But USA Network's *La Femme Nikita* is one of those rare movie-to-television spin-offs that has actually managed to surpass its progenitor, allowing this particular femme to join the ranks of the relatively few, among them the 4077th of *M*A*S*H*, Oscar Madison and Felix Unger of Neil Simon's *The Odd Couple,* and respective human and alien cops Matt Sikes and George Francisco from *Alien Nation.*

Nikita actually has quite a bit in common with such revolutionary cop shows as *Miami Vice* and *Wiseguy* in that it effortlessly manages to combine style with substance, pushing its filmic techniques as far as the medium will allow while never losing sight of its characters. The characters inhabiting the world of *Nikita* never really stand still, existing instead in a constant state of evolution.

From nearly the beginning of its run two seasons ago, the series was adopted as a darling of both the critics and the audience, becoming basic cable's highest-rated series and pulling in a weekly audience of about two million viewers. More important, it has triggered the type of fervent cult following that higher-rated shows—including such blockbusters as *ER* and *Friends*—can only dream of having.

La Femme Nikita X-Posed is the first guide written about the series, and as such it serves as an introduction to the show and the feature film that inspired it. Within these pages you'll find a complete guide to the first year-and-a-half of the series, an A-to-Z encyclopedia, voices of the cast and crew as culled from various magazine and Internet interviews, and the humorous "Idiot's Guide to Section One," which provides all the hints you'll need to survive in Nikita's world.

LA FEMME NIKITA X-POSED

Albert L. Ortega

chapter one

LA HISTORY
NIKITA

Although there's no denying the impact that USA's *La Femme Nikita* has had on audiences—elevating stars Peta Wilson and Roy Dupuis to cult-sensation status and making the series the highest-rated show on cable television—the bottom line is that Nikita owes her very existence to French filmmaker Luc Besson.

Currently developing a big-budget version of *Joan of Arc,* Besson most recently scored with the Bruce Willis science-fiction action adventure *The Fifth Element.*

"I make films that are neither art nor culture," Besson told *Scanorama.* "I am more fascinated by the possibility of films as fantasy. I want people to be swept away by the force of the images. Most French directors lather their films with endless talk. I try to let the visual take precedence so that you experience the film through your emotions."

He certainly accomplished that with 1990's *Nikita,* which Leonard Maltin referred to as "stylish and compelling, if not always believable."

In the film, released in America under the title *La Femme Nikita,* Besson's former wife, Anne Parillaud, is cast in the title role of a young punk drug addict who murders a cop and is sentenced to death. Instead of being executed, she is secretly retrained as an assassin by a previously unheard-of branch of the French police.

Interestingly, when viewed with a current perspective, it's fascinating to look at the Besson film to see just how far removed it and

> **"** Interestingly, when viewed with a current perspective, it's fascinating to look at the Besson film just to see just how far removed it and the television series are from each other. Beyond the fact that this Nikita is a killer, there is nothing about the covert government agency that suggests the realm or influence of Section One. **"**

the television series are from each other. Beyond the fact that this Nikita *is* a killer, there is nothing about the covert government agency of the French film that suggests the realm or influence of the Section One of the television series.

Certainly the ruthlessness of this agency is comparable to its TV counterpart, but the French Nikita exists in a world of shadow and grime, rather than that of the TV's oftentimes sterile high tech, completely suggesting an agency consisting of the dregs of society. Even when this Nikita is held in a white room, there is a grit to the place that belies the expected image. It's also rather intriguing to have the opportunity to look back at the character's origin, if you will.

In Anne Parillaud's hands, Nikita truly begins as a vicious killer; a member of society in self-imposed exile who leaves no doubt to the imagination that she deserves to die. And yet, as Nikita goes through her transformation from street punk to highly trained assassin, her humanity gradually begins to rise to the surface. By film's end you're doing the one thing that you never expected to be doing at the outset: rooting for Nikita and her vie for freedom and rebirth in the form of her new persona.

Probably one of the most powerful moments of the film is when Nikita unwittingly goes on her first assignment: assassinating a target in a very public restaurant. During this scene, director Besson paints an astounding contrast between life in "the Center," as the secret organization is called, and the opulence of France's upperclass. Parillaud does a marvelous job of taking in her surroundings with the wide-eyed innocence of a child visiting a strange new world. Interestingly, when Nikita kills her target and flees to a supposed restroom exit, she is suddenly back in her old world, with its urinals dirty and rusting and paint peeling off one of the walls. From there she's in back rooms, a kitchen, where she finally escapes through a garbage chute. Yet despite all of this, she seems to gain strength as she becomes more immersed in her old elements and her desperate struggle to stay alive.

Albert L. Ortega

Nikita director, Luc Besson— the man who started it all.

Much of the rest of the film is Nikita's internal conflict between living the new life that has been forced upon her, and the price that that chance continually exacts from her emotions and soul.

"I saw Nikita as a woman who has been drained of ordinary sentiment," said Besson. "I feel sad that many people wind up living lives that they don't want or can't change. That, for me, represents the essential tragedy of the human experience. So I thought of a story about a woman who is given a second chance at life. Nikita relearns everything about how to behave towards others, how to dress and look and how to love again."

Parillaud, also known to American audiences for her turn as a vampire in John Landis's *Innocent Blood* and seen most recently in *The Man in the Iron Mask*, made her starring film debut as Nikita, and she electrified critics and audiences alike with her performance. "[Luc Besson] brought out that strength, the rage in-

THE WISEGUY CONNECTION

Although *La Femme Nikita* has been deemed a highly original series, the one show it has been favorably compared to in tone is the Ken Wahl series, *Wiseguy*.

"Interestingly," Surnow told *Cinescape* magazine, "a lot of the same qualities and shadings that you find in *Wiseguy* you find in *Nikita*. The whole idea of a tortured soul is very important. You're dealing with a government operative who moves through a dangerous, violent world while trying to carve out and save a little piece of humanity for herself."

Notes Nikita herself, Peta Wilson, "The difference between *Nikita* and *Wiseguy* is that Vinnie Terranova *wanted* to be a cop, and Nikita is antiestablishment. It doesn't matter what they do, their actions speak louder than words."

In *Wiseguy*, which ran on CBS from 1987 to 1991, Wahl portrays undercover agent Terranova, who spent eighteen months in prison to help create his cover as a "wiseguy." Upon release, he begins a series of investigations that range from the mob and white supremacists to international arms dealers and ruthless music-industry power brokers.

The biggest difference between this show and nearly every other cop series of the time was the realism of its characters and situations—and the tense, visceral quality of the show. Whether you're talking about Terranova; his field director, Frank McPike (Jonathan Banks); or Lifeguard (*Highlander*'s Jim

side me. On the surface I look fragile and insecure; you have to know me very well. I try to live the moment and not obey laws, rules, conventions, or norms," she has said, sounding as though she could be talking about Nikita as well as herself. "[I try] to react to a sensation, a feeling or an emotion. You can't program emotion. I don't want to program my characters or choice of films. I want love to rule—love of a character, a film, work with a director—and love is unpredictable: You never know when you're going to fall in love. I have no game plan. Even if it's hard to live that way, it makes me feel alive. I listen to what goes on inside."

In fact, that attitude had resulted in Parillaud having a difficult time shaking the character after the cameras had stopped rolling. "For a while," she noted, "[Nikita] was in me like a

THE WISEGUY CONNECTION, continued

Byrnes), the behind-the-scenes operator who saved Vinnie on more than a couple of occasions, these really were guys you'd expect to meet in dark alleys and the backrooms of mob-run restaurants. Spicing up the drama was the shifting, unclear dividing line between good and evil, and the moments that made the audience wonder which side of the fence Vinnie would ultimately land on.

"That's the whole point of the series, to show that everybody's not all good, not all bad," said Wahl, who could easily be speaking about characters from *Nikita* as well. "These things intertwine and therein lies the conflict. It wasn't just Gene Autry riding into town with his white hat on. I must say that that's one of my favorite things about this character. He's an undercover agent, so *he's* acting. When you're an actor doing a part, you're not living in constant fear—well, I guess some actors are—but when this character is acting, there's a lot of underlying fear because he has to make sure he's saying the right thing all the time."

Unlike most episodic villains, the *Wiseguy* antagonists weren't dispatched after one or two episodes. Sometimes it took up to nine installments of a saga—or arc, as it was referred to by the show's creative team—for a tale to be resolved. "I knew as a writer that it would create a situation where Vinnie would be a counterpuncher as opposed to carrying the action in a story," cocreator Stephen J. Cannell told *Rolling Stone*. "My idea was that we would reinvent the show every six months."

(continued)

demon. I would do things I normally would not do. She was awkward, depressed, full of despair. But to me there was also a spiritual underline to Nikita. In a very excessive way she is a loudspeaker of the youth of society today. She destroys herself because she doesn't believe in anything on Earth. Such a role in the career of an actress is already enormous. But I didn't have an American Dream. My sensibility is thoroughly European. By my tongue, my emotions. I don't have a career plan. What counts is the character. I leave it alone to live within my interior self. My body becomes like an apartment in which the character is a tenant. It can change the furniture, the layout, the decoration. It does what it wants!"

And obviously the character of Nikita wanted to live beyond the con-

THE WISEGUY CONNECTION, continued

Joel Surnow had actually been offered the job of producer of the original series. "I think the reason they came to me," he mused, "is because I had come off of the first year of *Miami Vice* and the first year of *The Equalizer,* and in a way those shows were kind of like a prelude to *Wiseguy.* They were the edgy cop shows that took a single male-lead or double male-lead format and made it more realistic than *Starskey & Hutch.*"

Surnow recognizes that the series' unique process of evolving stories over several episodes provided much of the show's power. So his greatest challenge when he wrote the reunion movie was to find a way to maintain that slowly unfolding tension within a single two-hour format.

"To do it," he explained, "you have to cut some things and hang it really on one kind of an emotional idea. In this case, it's a relationship with a woman. There's all kinds of great stuff from the original show that's worked into the framework of the two hours. Vinnie does what he's always done, only it's ten years later and he's still doing it. This story is basically designed to recapture the spirit of the series. Actually, the spirit of the first year, which was wonderful. During that year, *Wiseguy* didn't really have to be about anything. It was simply about good, hard cop stuff spun out in an inventive, sometimes surreal world. The show never felt completely realistic to me. They were always pushing the envelope of what the audience would supposedly take. It went two clicks past it, and everybody loved what they did."

fines of Besson's cinematic vision. As Hollywood producer Art Linson related to journalist Steve Pond, "I saw *La Femme Nikita* in Seattle, and I immediately called [former Warner Bros. production president] Bruce Berman and said, 'God, Bruce, you guys should go out and get this movie. You could make a lot of money with this. I don't know if it's something *I* would wanna do, but this is a terrific movie and nobody's seeing it because audiences are too lazy to read subtitles. Just adapt it like a great play and put on another production of it.' And he said, 'Isn't that coincidental? We've already bought it. Do you want to produce it?'"

Linson agreed, with the directorial reins ultimately being given to John Badham, whose credits at that time included *Saturday Night Fever*, *Dracula*, *Wargames*, *Blue Thunder*, and *The Hard Way*.

THE WISEGUY CONNECTION, continued

Wiseguy was originally launched with a script by Cannell and Frank Lupo. According to Lupo, it was difficult to decide exactly where to start. "We had one draft that started when Vinnie first entered the bureau's training academy," he says, "and we had the one where he's in the middle of the scam that puts him in prison. I would say the first half hour of the show should have been the one that got him locked up, and that was the kind of material we were testing. But in a pilot, you have to give the network an idea of what the show will be like. Had we handed in these stories, the network would've said, 'Okay, this tells us that the series is coming, but not what the series will be.' By the time we were getting closer, working on the second story I mentioned, we felt it wasn't as far developed as the two hours that would eventually air. Then we said, 'You know, we've got to keep going, we should either write a three-hour pilot or short-cut the front end.' We short-cut the front end, with the intent of always being able to do a flashback one day; a flashback which reveals how he went to OCB [Organized Crime Bureau] training and then to prison."

In the aired pilot, Vinnie has been released from prison and hooks up with mob kingpin Sonny Steelgrave (the late Ray Sharkey). As the federal agent digs himself deeper into the Steelgrave organization, a brotherly relationship develops between the two men. By the time the story reaches its apex, it has become obvious that doing the "right" thing could be difficult for Vinnie. In a sense, betraying Sonny would be like betraying himself.

(continued)

"The original *Nikita* was very marginally successful in the United States," Badham claimed. "The truth is that Americans will not go to see a picture in a language that is not English. And you can forget subtitles. It's kind of that way in other parts of the world, too, which is why we dub into French, Spanish, Italian, and even Japanese. So here's this fabulous movie and a great story. I'm watching it and saying, 'You know, this is going to die. Nobody's going to see this movie. It would make a wonderful American version, and if I'm seeing it here at the Beverly Center in Hollywood, other people have seen this long before me and they've probably got the same idea.'

"Sure enough," he continues, "Warner Bros. had already jumped on it and were ready to do it. I went over there and said, 'Listen, I'd like to try

THE WISEGUY CONNECTION, continued

"We wanted to come up with a character that Vinnie could truly admire on the other side of the fence," Lupo says. "And as the whole Sonny Steelgrave story started, it was almost like a miniseries rather than a television pilot. We knew we were going to build up the relationship between Vinnie and Sonny so that by the time we hit the end, it wouldn't be a situation where Sonny is arrested and Vinnie, with a tear in his eye, says, 'We got you, asshole.' Needless to say, this kind of thing raised a few eyebrows at CBS, and they said to us, 'Couldn't Vinnie really be faking Sonny Steelgrave out? He doesn't have to *truly* admire him.' We said, 'You don't understand where we're coming from,' and their response was, 'It's going to be really clear that Vinnie's not going over, right?' We said, 'We're not sure. We will redeem him, but it has got to be enticing.' So it was that kind of reaction, but there wasn't a tremendous amount of resistance."

"I love the character," added executive producer David Burke, who guided the series as Surnow guides *Nikita*. "I thought the relationship between Vinnie and Sonny was one Vinnie would like to maintain as a friendship, but he can't because he knows the true stripes of the man. That was enticing. I'm not a big fan of gunplay, and *Wiseguy* presented the opportunity to actually spend time with characters and develop them fully. I think one of our greatest strengths was that we were able to give actors material they could really sink their teeth into. That, for me, was the essential strength of what we did, and we and make the American version of this.' They said, 'We hired Luc Besson, he was going to do the American version but then he woke up one day and said, "Wait a second, I did this already."' He had the good sense that he didn't want to do a remake. It's too hard to make a movie anyway, but then to have to go through it again just to change the language is an exercise in exhaustion. So they turned to me and said, 'Go ahead.' That's how we got to that point on it.

"I just liked the character," Badham notes of the appeal of the project, "and thought she was marvelous. I liked the transformation of a non-socialized creature, [a] totally sociopathic, feral, wild thing into a human being. I thought that was quite fascinating. And how she dealt with the world around her and as she began to

THE WISEGUY CONNECTION, continued

were real fortunate with performers, people who weren't afraid to play big moments and to play dialogue that is not traditional television."

Among the actors drawn to the series were Kevin Spacey, Joan Severence, Fred Dalton Thompson (now a U.S. senator from Tennessee), Jerry Lewis, Ron Silver, Tim Curry, Paul Winfield, and Robert Davi. With such talent, along with first-rate rating, *Wiseguy* gained enormous cult status—but the ratings lingered in the lower half of the Nielsen lists, and the show struggled through three seasons. Then Wahl and Cannell had a falling-out regarding the future direction of the show, resulting in the star departing. *Something* was obviously wrong because when *Wiseguy* returned for its fourth season, Steven Bauer had been cast in the new lead role of Michael Santana and the entire original writing staff had departed. On camera, Vinnie was believed dead, victim of an international drug cartel. With little fanfare, the series disappeared a handful of episodes later.

"His death was left ambiguous on the show," says Surnow, "but the reunion movie didn't deal with that at all. As far as we're concerned, it's just ten years later for the characters. I love the show and, not to toot my own horn, this script is like the *real* show. It's like first-year *Wiseguy* with the appropriate updating. The characters don't communicate with codes the way they used to. Also, the OCB isn't the

(continued)

realize what she was doing and how she wanted to pull away from it. I loved the idea of having an action hero that was a woman, but it was not a tough, Amazon-like person, but someone who had great beauty and femininity."

The film was ultimately retitled *Point of No Return,* and Bridget Fonda was cast in the lead—a role, Badham points out, that virtually every actress, no matter the age, wanted. His feeling, though, was that the part would have to go to someone young. "You can almost excuse what she does at the beginning of the movie if she's eighteen or nineteen," he says, "but if you start getting into the mid-twenties, it starts

looking like she's got a real serious problem. It's like casting Diana Ross in *The Wiz.*"

"This is a tough part," Linson told *Premiere* magazine. "It's a girl who starts out as a drugged-out, down-and-out cop killer and gets completely changed. And when you start at that level, you have to have the kind of actress you care about, who can pull you in so you say, 'I know what she did, but I really like her.' And that's ultimately why we went with Bridget."

"It was fun," adds Badham, "because there's Bridget who's a very intelligent, sweet, gentle person with a lot of strength underneath, so there's a very strong woman there, too. She

THE WISEGUY CONNECTION, continued

same. The Young Turks have taken over the agency and have sort of made Vinnie one of the dinosaurs from the old era."

In the movie, Vinnie went undercover in Silicon Valley. "What I tried to do was figure out where you can make more money than the drug trade," Surnow says. "Silicon Valley is the answer, especially the illegal use of the Internet through the World Wide Web. There's a tremendous opportunity there for ill-gotten gains, and it's the perfect assignment for Vinnie Terranova."

Although there probably won't be any future *Wiseguy* movies, fans can take heart from the fact that Surnow has claimed he hopes *Nikita,* in its third season, will tackle a few arc-like storylines.

was able to give us both sides of the character."

For her part, Fonda notes, "I hate American remakes. I think they usually take great foreign movies and lobotomize them and take out everything that made them good in the first place. But let's face it, where else am I gonna be offered a role that lets me do the kind of things this one does? I *had* to take it."

Unfortunately, *Point of No Return* was not everything Fonda had hoped it would be. Badham and company unwisely elected to stay *so* close to the original that many of the sequences are staged exactly the same, although the Besson original devoted considerably more time to atmosphere, subtle character nuances, and a general grittiness that is missing here. Generally speaking, this film is a sanitized remake that pales in comparison because so much of it leaves the audience no choice but to compare the two versions.

> **Despite the fact that La Femme Nikita didn't score at the box office, its premise remained a potent one, and it seemed ideal for the USA Network, which was attempting to establish a reputation for itself.**

While Fonda does her best in the role, she *just* misses bringing the raw power to Nikita that Parillaud did. Probably the best analogy would be to the James Bond series when George Lazenby stepped in for Sean Connery in 1969's *On Her Majesty's Secret Service,* giving us an adequate enough performance but choosing to mirror Connery in as many ways as possible. This differed from Roger Moore's becoming 007, when he—whether you liked his interpretation or not—molded the character to suit his own strengths as an actor. One can't help but feel that Fonda is merely going through the paces in an attempt to imitate her

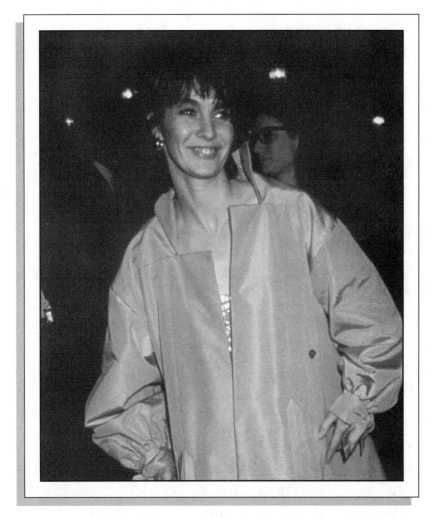

Albert L. Ortega

Anne Parilland—the first actress
to take on the role of Nikita.

out, "I thought, if we stay kind of true to it and Americanize it in a smart way, it could be worthwhile, knowing that you're just putting your head on the chopping block to make a movie so soon after something that was so good."

Notes Badham, "We tried to say, 'What do we do differently? What do we add?' And we knew there was stuff in there that if we didn't include, people would kill us. Can we improve on things? It's always really dangerous to go into something like that that people will have seen and will be comparing you to. You're really taking your life in your hands, and then you wake up one morning and read reviews that tell you what a horrible person you are. The film worked for a lot of people, and didn't for others."

predecessor, without providing any original characterization.

Everyone involved knew the risk of remaking *Nikita,* with Linson pointing

Despite the fact that *La Femme Nikita* didn't score at the box office, its premise remained a potent one, and it seemed ideal for the USA Network, which was attempting to establish a reputation for itself with innovative original programming. Certainly the USA Network had dabbled in originals, first with the anthologies *The Hitchhiker, Ray Bradbury Theatre,* and the remake of *Alfred Hitchcock Presents,* and then with the *Weird Science* spin-off of the feature film of the same name. They went darker with *Matrix,* and then attempted to tackle science fiction with William Shatner's *TekWar,* a weekly version of the TV movies that had been airing in first-run syndication.

La Femme Nikita, however, would be their most ambitious effort to date. Rod Perth, president of USA Network, last year detailed, "I loved the [Luc Besson] movie. I felt that it could be a series. There was a French company that owned the rights, because they

> **"** I think we kind of just fell into this really strange, rhythmic, moody piece that we didn't necessarily know we were creating when we put all the elements together. **"**
>
> —Executive consultant Joel Surnow

owned the feature film. We worked with them and then it went through various stages. We ended up with the current production arrangement we have, which is based in Toronto. We got a script from [*Nikita* executive consultant] Joel Surnow that we thought had real potential. Most importantly, it was a show that simply was not on television."

It was also a show that had certain "issues" attached to it that had to be dealt with before it could go forward.

"USA had done a show [*Matrix*] a couple of years before that had a very dark lead," explained Joel Surnow. "They were nervous about *Nikita* being too dark. USA said, 'If you have a woman who is a killer and ends up being brought into the organization and kills, it's too dark.' I had to agree with them. I felt like the character from the movie couldn't sustain as a TV series character because she killed a cop in cold blood while high on drugs. I felt I couldn't bring her into my house week after week and just really root for her. So I pitched USA the idea of making her an innocent who was at the wrong place at the wrong time, and then has to survive by pretending to be the person she isn't. By making her innocent, suddenly she's any one of us who's caught up in a nightmare like that. It's even more poignant that she comes out of the 'program' after all this training, and isn't aware that they had found out she was innocent but didn't do anything about it because she's so talented and special. She is eternally trying to get out of this situation and have a real life for herself, but can't. They have a hold on her, a sort of blackmail. I call this show an action tragedy.

"She wouldn't be an assassin," he added. "She will be killing, but that's not her job. She'll kill just as if a cop would kill if he had to. Nikita is probably the first time on television that you have a female action hero. It's not *Police Woman* where she's more cerebral. She's actually twisting guys' necks and kicking and shooting and killing. It's a real person. It's a James Cameron female action hero, like Linda Hamilton in the *Terminator* films or Ripley from *Alien.*"

Surnow admitted that, at the beginning of the series, there was some concern on the network's part about American audiences possibly not responding to complex international spy stories. "They like their crime stories neat," he mused. "You know, 'He's the bad guy, he's hurting this person, go get him.' When it gets into La Carre territory with 'Who's the good guy and who's the bad guy in this shadowy, gray world?' some people tune out. What we've tried to do are visceral CIA stories. Like hostage situations, terrorists and international drug dealers— just on a bigger scale, but still accessible and morally unambiguous. We also enjoy doing undercover material. I think we have to use the fact that this is a young, beautiful woman and the last person you'd think who would go into the world of terrorists, or whatever. I think we can use the unexpectedness of her being this lethal weapon."

In an online chat, series story editor Michael Loceff noted, "Nikita is, first and foremost, an emotional being. Her strength to Section One is that while she is a capable operative, she persists in displaying this emotional fabric. It results in creative solutions to tactical problems but also leaves her vulnerable to certain manipulation. As the [series] progresses, she will demonstrate strong counter-aspects to her personality. In season one we discovered the 'down-the-middle' Nikita. Season two [explores] some more exotic parts of her psyche at both ends of the spectrum, but her emotional center of gravity will not change."

Albert L. Ortega

Bridget Fonda was the American version of Nikita.

Based on the pilot episode of the series, simply titled "Nikita," it's obvious

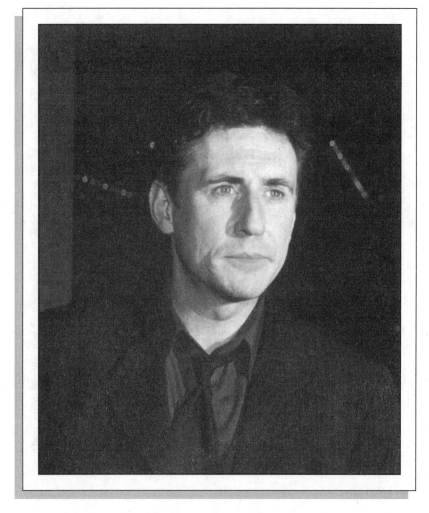

Albert L. Ortega

Gabriel Byrne portrayed Nikita's "mentor" in John Badham's American remake, <u>Point of No Return.</u>

ultimate high-tech anti-terrorist organization. Their members, led by Operations (Eugene Glazer) and Madeline (Alberta Watson), and even Nikita's "contact," Michael (Roy Dupuis), are far more ruthless than anyone represented in Section's earlier incarnation. These people seem soulless and spend a great deal of time proving that (although fans will be shocked to see Michael actually raise his voice and Madeline betray a bit of compassion for Nikita in this episode).

"They're really Machiavellian and cold to the core," Surnow has said. "They're almost without souls, but if you look at them deep enough, you think, 'They do have souls, they just suppress them.' Someone wrote an interesting article about us; about our

that there are quite a few changes from the feature film. First off, Section One replaces Besson's Center, and it is a beyond-state-of-the-art facility; the show being analogous to the workplace. They said they could relate to the show because it's like the workplace: Your boss asks you to do unruly things, you're stuck in your job, and so on. It was an interesting comparison."

The real standout, of course, is former-model-turned-actress Peta Wilson, who is electrifying as Nikita. Unlike Bridget Fonda in *Point of No Return*, she took the role and immediately made it her own. Even in the restaurant scene—which on a surface level becomes painfully boring when you watch Besson's *Nikita, Point of No Return,* and the pilot, one after another—she provides some fresh wrinkles despite the tiredness of the action sequence itself. Wilson's Nikita, unlike Parillaud's and Fonda's, never does sort of get into the moment, choosing *not* to become more powerful as the action unfolds. From the very beginning, she proclaims that she's not a killer; and it's something that the actress never loses sight of. In a sense, it becomes the grounding aspect of the character, which, in turn, allows for all of the events around her to be both poignant

and repugnant. Quite simply, this is a role that Wilson was born to play.

"We had a casting session in my office," said Perth, "and she was just spectacular. We knew we had a star."

And it was the vulnerability of that star that gave the series so much creative juice in the beginning, as Nikita struggled to make the best of her situation while simultaneously trying to come up with a way out. As such, the character is constantly walking a tightrope between her emotions and her obligation to Section One. That becomes apparent in the episode "Charity," in which she gets too close to her target, a supposed money launderer who also happens to run a charity for troubled children. Only after Nikita falls in love with him does she come to realize that he is actually head of a child slave-labor ring and that he has to be brought down.

In "Love," she begins an exploration of her complex feelings for Michael as they pose as a married couple in an effort to stop an international arms smuggler. She can't help but be struck by the irony that the man she is falling

Albert L. Ortega

```
Dermot Mulroney was the
American Nikita's love interest.
```

by coming to the aid of his wife.

The early episodes of the series also highlight Nikita's efforts to lead something of an ordinary life outside of Section, while simultaneously she is being constantly manipulated by those around her. "I think our dumping shit on Nikita is what keeps the audience interested," Surnow told *Retro-Vision Online.* "Let's face it, Peta Wilson is so strong, that if you don't do that to her she wouldn't be likable. She's incredibly aggressive, she does action better than any woman on TV or film and she's just so tough. It's breaking her down that keeps her likable."

in love with is also one of the people keeping her "prisoner" in Section. Things become even more confusing in "Simone" as she actually *helps* Michael

In "Friend," Nikita thinks she's helping an old childhood friend, who turns out to actually be an operative on assignment; in "Treason" she is torn between the mission at hand and trying to turn things around so she can save an operative's son, who is being held hostage. A real turning point, however, occurs in "Mother" when Nikita has to go undercover and pretend to be the long-lost daughter of a woman who, along with her husband, is in possession of a nuclear trigger. Beyond Nikita's fervent wish that she had had a relationship with her real mother that was anywhere near as strong as the one she has with this woman, there is, at last, a certain acceptance of her life in Section. In fact, at the end of this episode she doesn't protest the fact that this woman is going to be killed by Section One, only that they let the woman die believing that she had finally found her daughter.

As Surnow said, "It's like Nikita is becoming part of the program. If this was the first or second episode it would have been, 'How could you do this?' so it's a real evolvement of the character. You know, the show kept being called *La Femme Nikita,* but we kind of went away from leading with her character and took in the whole idea that it's Section One that's interesting about this show. She's the dominant part of it and we see it through her, but it's not about the life of this girl anymore. It's about the life of these people and this girl is the prominent one. Yet she remains our emotional connection and our eyes and ears to it all. She's sort of our moral compass."

"Escape" continues her manipulation by Michael. She has the chance for freedom but refuses to take it because he confesses his supposed feelings for her; and then, after she changes her mind, he reveals that he was lying.

A character always in evolution, Nikita strikes out on her own emotionally with her relationship with architect Gray Wellman in the episodes "Gray" and "Choice." Again, to show that this isn't like most series on the air, "Gray" ends with Nikita and Wellman having dinner, while Michael spies on them from across the street. Let's face it, the majority of shows *won't* have one of its heroes pulling double duty as a peeping Tom. "Choice" also moves back to Nikita's roots a bit with a key scene from the Besson feature, in which she is ordered to kill someone from a bathroom window, with her boyfriend just on the other side of the bathroom door.

"Rescue" provides a twist on things. Nikita and Madeline actually have to rescue Michael, who's been injured in a Soviet-bloc country (and Madeline actually induces a heart attack to get them into the hospital they believe he's in).

In some ways, "Innocent" is a throwback to earlier episodes, with Nikita protecting a mentally challenged man named Rudy, who was witness to a nuclear-bomb transfer. "We'd played her wanting-to-get-out-of-the-Section card for the first seven episodes pretty heavily," Surnow said in another online interview, "and along the way we learned that one of the best places to put her is protecting an innocent person. We wanted her to protect the most innocent person in the world, which would be this kind of grown-up child. Nikita looks good doing that. There was beginning to be too much self-centeredness in the show: 'I've got to get out,' and so on. One of

the things I learned from [the UPN series] *Nowhere Man* is that although the audience can relate to 'me, me, me,' it doesn't make you heroic; and at the end of the day, I think your series' leads have to be heroic on some level."

"Gambit" is the beginning of the effort to explore some of the other characters, with Madeline spending most of the episode involved in a *Silence of the Lambs*-type conversation with an international terrorist that is riveting to watch. Two episodes later, following "Recruit," "Obsessed" puts Michael firmly in the spotlight, manipulating an abused woman for the Section's ends. Operations is next up for "star" status, in "Missing," dealing with Nikita's efforts to retrieve his long-lost son, Steven, from the ranks of a criminal organization; and hacker expert Birkoff (Matthew Ferguson) demonstrates his inability to deal with the world outside of Section in "Noise," quite literally putting his life at risk.

The aforementioned "Recruit" represents the next step in Nikita's "career," as she ascends the ladder of Section success. Operatives have started being placed beneath her in rank, and she begins having to make the same kind of cold-blooded decisions she's witnessed since the show's beginning.

"Voices" is intriguing in that a bit of the real world enters the scene as Section is forced to work to some degree with the police. At the same time, Nikita gets to kick a rapist's ass, which is eminently satisfying for both her and the audience.

Section operatives are captured in "War," an episode that, beyond the evident torture, begins a full-blown exploration of Michael's and Nikita's feelings for each other. While the follow-up, "Verdict," is a straight-ahead action episode, "Brainwashed" is an almost science-fiction entry that pushes the high-tech aspect of the series to its furthest degree but maintains its grasp on reality,

Albert L. Ortega

Harvey Keitel portrayed the "cleaner" in <u>Point of No Return.</u>

thanks to Nikita's exorcism of personal demons and addiction to a mind device.

Season one ended with "Mercy," a startling episode in the sense that

Operations, believing that Nikita's rebellious spirit has gone too far, sends her on a suicide mission, from which Michael, amazingly, saves her. At episode's end, she secretly has her freedom, while Section One believes that she's dead.

La Femme Nikita's second season is barely into its run at the time of this writing, though what can be determined is that Nikita ultimately returns to Section and many of the episodes will be devoted to the continued exploration of her relationship with Michael as well as her evolution as a character. Said story editor Michael Loceff in an online chat, "We will see certain aspects of Section One this season and go deeper into how it works, who makes decisions, plans missions, handles contingencies. You will see Michael give more information about himself (in homeopathic quantities, of course), and you will see Nikita take some interesting growth spurts."

Elsewhere, Surnow observed, "Nikita is absolutely no less headstrong or independent [in the second season], though she did open up her heart to Michael this season, which made her more vulnerable when she returned to Section. She quickly made an adjustment when she realized that this relationship was not going to continue. But from now on, you'll see a cannier, more savvy and smarter Nikita than we've ever seen before. Her survival instincts have kicked into overdrive."

In a separate interview, Surnow noted that he remains completely jazzed about this series. "I think we kind of just fell into this really strange, rhythmic, moody piece that we didn't necessarily know we were creating when we put all the elements together," he said. "What this show has that *Wiseguy* had that I love about shows is that it deals with real power; people in real seats of power dealing with global things. It's not about local bad guys. It's about people doing things that can change the face of civilization. If you look at our show, it never really takes place in mundane places. It's always subterranean or remote parts of the world; pockets of places that don't look or feel familiar. And the people that combat them, Section One, is sort of an invisible, underground organization, and the people they're fighting against are off the prosaic. There's this thin layer of society that nobody really sees, but which nonetheless has really tremendous power and is tremendously dangerous. That's always exciting to me because it allows you to have a lot of leeway to do a lot of crazy stuff, and you're able to assume that people that powerful are simply dangerous. If there's anything about the show that's more feature film-like, it's that. It goes against a bigger canvas than most shows."

chapter two

LA STAR
NIKITA

My role models weren't from television," proclaims actress Peta Wilson, star of USA's *La Femme Nikita.* "I liked Angie Dickenson in *Police Woman,* but mine came from history. You know, from studying Joan of Arc . . . there are so many, even the queens of England. Shakespeare wrote great women. So I think, generally, my role models haven't come from television, they've come from history books and my mother."

It's not exactly what one would expect to hear from one of the tube's sexiest, most lethal heroines; but then again, there isn't much that one could anticipate from Wilson. That was certainly the impression of Joel Surnow, who was surprised to find that the third actress who read for the role—Wilson—was perfect, despite the fact he had another 197 people to audition.

"Peta grew up in the wilds of New Guinea and part of her has never left," Surnow, who guides the weekly spin-off, told the press. "She's got this incredible combination of rawness, vulnerability, sensuality and unpredictability—equal parts of all four of those things. It's a very tough part to play and you've got to be a lot of different things. She is. We read 200 different women and there wasn't even a close second.

"Nikita has got to have the physicality to be an operative, a lethal weapon, yet at the same time this is a girl who *wasn't* a killer," Surnow explained. "She's got to bring to it some heroism and real human appeal. Like *Wiseguy,* we're trying to disguise a drama show as an action show. You have to use an actor with those chops, and she has them. What's surprising to me is that she's never done anything on film before, yet she's adapted to the medium beautifully."

Peta Gia Wilson, the daughter of retired warrant officer Darcy Wilson and caterer Karlene Wilson, was born on November 11, 1970, in Sydney, Australia. Of her unusual name, Wilson has explained, "I've been a tomboy, so I wanted people to call me 'Pete.' I was always kind of short. My father was away in the bush on an army exercise when my mum had me. The message to my father was wrong. They said I was a boy, so he came into town looking for a boy. My dad wanted to call me 'Peter.' My mom didn't want that, but the name stuck. My father called me Peter. I hated my name. I wanted a name like Tanya, Louise or Sarah. But I've had a voice like I always had and a name like Peta. At nine, I had a husky voice. I changed my name every two weeks. My grandmother would ask me a question in my name, but I wouldn't answer. My grandfather would have to tell her my name for the week. But now it's my name. People have such problems saying it, though. Also, 1970 Miss Australia was Peta. I think that had something to do with it as well."

Raised in Papua New Guinea, where there was no television, she and her brother started performing shows for family and friends for entertainment. This self-described army brat traveled often while growing up, another factor that played no small part in fostering her love for acting.

"When I was five years old," she says, "and living in New Guinea, we didn't have any television. I went to Australia to visit my grandparents. Remember the show *I Dream of Jeannie?* I had an outfit just like hers and I came back to the native people of New Guinea, who had given me such wonderful things, and I'd put on these shows and be Jeannie."

She was also guided by her family's mobility, preventing development of long-term relationships, which meant she had to adapt quickly, sizing up so-

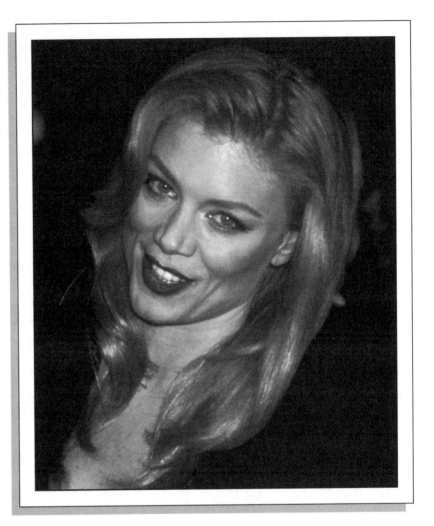

Albert L. Ortega

Peta Wilson has effortlessly made
the role of Nikita her own.

cial situations and doing whatever would help her rapidly fit in. Ironically, it was the perfect training ground for essaying the role of Nikita; a role she was hired for, six years after moving to America.

As she grew up, Wilson engaged herself in sports, particularly basketball and sailing. "I love sports," she enthused online. "It kept me out of trouble. It gave me energy, and sports was a place to put it. Now, acting is the place to put it. I was not a pro basketball player in Australia. I was a professional Net player. It's different. You don't dribble. I would hate to get on the court with a champion basketballer. Net ball and basketball are different, like soccer and rugby."

Of sailing, she added, "Trailer Sailor is a boat, a sail boat, that you can tow in a trailer on the back of your car. And we had a Corsair, which is like a dingy [sic]. It's a racing boat. And we actually had the heaviest boat in the fleet. It was

ROY DUPUIS (MICHAEL)

Although *La Femme Nikita* is an ensemble drama, the lion's share of attention undoubtedly goes to Peta Wilson's Nikita and Roy Dupuis's Michael, the enigmatic Section One operative.

"My casting person showed me a head-shot of Roy," reflects executive consultant Joel Surnow. "She said, 'This actor was just submitted for the part of Michael.' My first impression was, 'This is exactly how I imagined Michael would look.' But I was skeptical because I hadn't seen his work or heard of him. We took a look at some of his film, including *Screamers* and *Million Dollar Babies,* and flew him down. I was sitting in my office waiting for Roy [who was coming] with Alberta Watson. When I looked out the window and saw Roy and Alberta, I knew I had my cast."

Born in Ontario, Canada, and raised in Quebec, Dupuis's first love was science, which lasted until he saw the film *Moliere.* So powerful was this film's impact that he went to school the next day and shifted his major from physics to theater.

American audiences came to know him when he starred as Oliva Dionne in the CBS miniseries *Million Dollar Babies,* the story of the Dionne quintuplets. He has appeared in such theatrical productions as *Romeo and Juliet* and *Harold and Maude,* on Canadian television in the series *Les Filles De Caleb* and such feature films as *Hemoglobin, Screamers, Jesus of Montreal, Being at Home With Claude,* and *Emily* and its sequel, *Blanche.*

It is, however, his role of Michael that has had the most impact on audiences, due largely to the sexual tension between him and Nikita, as well as the character's economy of words, doing much of his emoting through his eyes.

"I start by reading the scenario," Dupuis told Box Top Live. "And each character has their own demands. Like Michael, for me, was mostly a lot of observation and inner feeling and a lot of logic and understanding." In explaining how he is able to keep the character's emotions in check, he added, "By understanding the Section, what it's all about. By understanding what Michael's all about, how he survived. The fact that he doesn't show emotions is because he wants to survive in there. All he's got left is life. It's a lot of concentration. Michael is always very focused and doesn't do any movement for nothing. Very minimalist. That was a choice that I made for this character. I don't even know if I made the choice or the character did. My favorite thing about Michael's personality is that he's a very intelligent character. It's fun to play intelligent people. The mystery of this character is fun to play, too. I hope he's fun to watch."

In comparing himself to Michael, Dupuis noted there are similarities and differences. The big one? "I don't think I could pull the trigger on anybody right now," he said in the same broadcast interview. "I used to hunt when I was younger. Today I don't let anybody hunt on my land . . . Once you play a character, you put a lot of yourself in it. It's hard for me to explain exactly what is part of me and what is not."

called *Bewitched*. And my father had the youngest crew. Me and my brother and three other kids. And me and my brother were the only ones that knew what we were doing. The other kids were just sort of in the boat for weight. My father was in command and I was the first mate. I worked the spinnaker. It was great. We were third across the line among five hundred boats. We capsized three times. And we were third over the line in the heaviest boat in the squadron by a lot. We also won the top/bottom trophy, which was a toilet seat, because we capsized the most."

Her entry into the nonsports professional world was as a model. "I actually made a living as a model for about seven years," she pointed out. "I did magazine work, Levi's, commercials, preg-

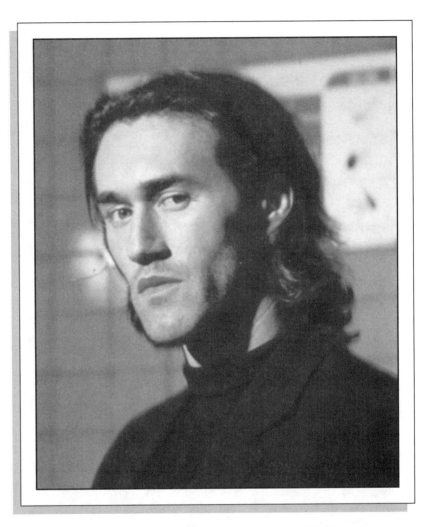

USA Network/Shooting Star

Roy Dupuis as the enigmatic Michael, Nikita's mentor in the Section and object of sexual tension.

nant catalogues with rubber stomachs. I got hired a lot because people seemed to like me, not because I was the prettiest girl in the room. I did a lot of

USA Network/Shooting Star

As Nikita, Peta Wilson manages
to encapsulate both sex and violence.

swimwear. The idea of studying acting just came to me when I was twenty-one. I figured, 'What do I have to lose?' I tried the hardest thing first. I came to America and came to drama schools. While others were partying, I would study. I would do the work. And then it just came. I got a manager through a girlfriend. He wouldn't take me on because he wanted real actors. I was scared and not ready to audition, so I ran out of there. But I auditioned for *Jade* [the film that would ultimately team David Caruso with Linda Florentino] and got four callbacks. *That* was enough for him to sign me. Six to seven months later, I got *Nikita.* Even after *Nikita* I was in drama school studying. I might go back to class during the hiatus if there is nothing interesting that comes along. So that's how I got my break. Just work. If you want to be an actor, just study hard. You have to have luck in there."

Referring to aspiring actors, she continued, "No one can use the excuse, 'If I just had an agent.' If actors want to act, they should act. If you study hard and work hard, work will come—and don't be discouraged. Try to learn as much as you can. Read a lot. It stimulates your senses. And try and listen. Listen to people and watch them. Try and observe. Keep your ego out of the

EUGENE ROBERT GLAZER (OPERATIONS)

Calling the shots on *La Femme Nikita* (or all that Nikita doesn't work her way around) is Operations, portrayed by Eugene Robert Glazer, who is *so* distinctly different from his on-screen persona that it can be shocking to people.

Hailing from New York, Glazer was born and raised in Brooklyn and spent his youth chasing footballs and women. His attention turned to acting when he began feeling burned out from working on Wall Street, where he traded over-the-counter securities.

Once he decided what he wanted to do, Glazer began pursuing acting with Operations-like determination. He managed to score stage roles in *Dylan*, *The Crucible*, *Lunchtime*, and *Staccato*; television appearances on *Quincy*, *Charlie's Angels*, *E.N.G.* and such TV movies as *Golden Will: The Silken Laumann Story*, *Women of Windsor*, and *The Substitute*, as well as feature films *Harlem Nights*, *Skeletons*, *Stepping Out*, *Hollywood Shuffle*, and *The Five Heartbeats*.

On *Nikita*, Operations is often at odds with la femme. "I don't hate her," Glazer explained during an online chat. "I don't like her attitude in dealing with certain situations. I feel she is one of the best operatives we have and I will allow her certain mistakes . . . but to a point.

"He's an enigmatic character who shows absolutely nothing to no one," Glazer adds. "Which doesn't mean that there's not a lot going on inside of him. But whatever it is . . . it's no one's business except his. He has to keep a certain distance from everyone in order to carry out the job at hand. From the executive producer, I was told that all of the characters are going to have more of the layers peeled back. . . . They want the audience to see a bit more of what drives these people."

way. Stay focused. Don't let anyone ever break your spirit. Don't give your talent away. Own it. Own what it is that makes you special. There are teachers out there who are very frustrated actors and sometimes they hurt young talent."

Wilson actually began her career in the local theater. She had been audition-

ing for films for seven months and had come close to a few features but inevitably lost out each time to "name" actresses. She was ready to head to New York and the theater circuit. "I said to my manager, 'I don't want to sit in L.A. and be like every other actress waiting for a break playing a handbag in a very commercial film. I'd rather go to New

ALBERTA WATSON (MADELINE)

As described in *Nikita*'s original press release, Madeline serves as Section One's master strategist, specializing in the emotional and psychological aspects of missions, and probing the psyches of operatives and opponents, "designing strategies that are most likely to succeed."

A native of Canada, Watson dropped out of school at the age of fifteen to join a Toronto theater company. From there she moved to New York, then to Los Angeles, and finally, after becoming convinced that life in the East was more educational and challenging, back to New York, where she spent a total of fourteen years.

She has starred in numerous TV movies, among them *Frame Up, Dog Hermit, Mood Indigo, Real Earth, White Earth*, and the miniseries *Kane & Abel*; guest-starred in such series as *The Outer Limits, Law & Order, The Equalizer*, and *Hill Street Blues*. Her big screen credits include the feature films *The Sweet Hereafter, Hackers, Spanking the Monkey, The Keep, Exposure, In Praise of Older Women, Seeds of Doubt*, and *Shoemaker*.

Of casting Watson as Madeline, executive consultant Joel Surnow noted online, "Alberta has a very compelling combination of ruthlessness, compassion, and sensuality."

For her part, Watson points out that the character's most difficult aspect to get a handle on is the sometimes nonstop stream of technobabble that is required. "She's like a cyborg," explains the actress of Madeline. "She gets her job done no matter what she has to do. Her outward appearance is civil and respectful, but she wouldn't think twice about ripping someone's heart out."

York and do theater. I love it and maybe I'll be "found" that way.'" She remained in L.A. only at the insistence of her agent, who recommended she try television.

"He said, 'Please would you consider going up for television?' and I said, 'I don't think I'm that kind of actress,'" Wilson reflected "The reason I felt that way is that I had so much energy. But I went up for three shows and was offered all three. One was a western, one was a sitcom, and the other was *Nikita*. I thought, 'Gee, at the point I'm at as an actress as far as not knowing so much technically, it may be better for me to be in a role that's close to me.'"

"I had five or six meetings, then seven meetings," Wilson says of the process she underwent for the role. "I had to audition for the heads of different networks and studios and it sort of finished off with me doing a film test

> **"** Wilson actually began her career in the local theater. She had been auditioning for films for seven months and had come close to a few features, but inevitably lost out each time to 'name' actresses. She was ready to head to New York and the theater circuit. . . . She remained in LA only at the insistence of her agent, who recommended she try television. **"**

on a sitcom set at Warner Bros. with all the executives sitting up in the stalls asking me questions, with all these lights on me. I felt like I was being interrogated. It was sort of more of what I thought the show was. I thought it was kind of a trick question, but it was more about trying to understand where they would go with it.

"I had no reference points," she elaborates. "My hat comes off to USA for taking a risk with me—a complete unknown actress who had very little experience on camera, and for the show itself. I'm pleasantly surprised, because coming from the theater, for me I had to sort of put all the stuff that I'd learned away and just live in the moment. The lack of time doesn't really afford me the opportunity to do the sort of work I like to do in terms of prep. Fortunately I know the character very well. It's been a great learning experience for me because every week I have to learn something new. They're very different mediums, television, film and theater. When I first started, I thought, 'It's all acting and should be treated the same way.' Well, that's not really the case in this medium because it's very technical, craftlike and sometimes it feels, in doing it, fake. Whereas the theater is very real. When I got reviews and stuff, I was pleasantly surprised by the positive ones. The negative ones didn't really bother me because I thought if I was doing everything that I wanted to do and was able to do, and then was judged negatively, then it would upset me. I know that I'm using as much as I can in this medium. I'm nicely surprised.

"I have some control of my performance, but [the network] is thinking of an audience. They will give me notes about what they want and what they don't want. Now instead of being frus-

MATTHEW FERGUSON (BIRKOFF)

If it involves computers in Section One, then Birkoff is the man of the moment: the ultimate rebel-hacker.

Actor Matthew Ferguson was born and raised on Toronto Island (population 700) in Canada. At the age of five, Ferguson first drew public attention to himself as part of a human chain designed to block government bulldozers from turning their community into a park (the effort worked, incidentally).

A graduate of the Claude Watson School for the Performing Arts, Ferguson's first role was on stage as Morgan Moreen in *Geometry in Venice*. He has appeared in such TV series as *PSI Factor*, *Street Legal*, and *Top Cops;* the feature films *The Long Kiss Goodnight*, *The English Patient*, *Eclipse,* and *Human Remains;* and the Showtime movies *Harrison Bergeron* and *The Deliverance of Elaine.*

trated about it, I say, 'Let me see what I can do within the square they're giving me.' That's the challenge, to still make it work even if I disagree or think it should be something else. Joel Surnow is the producer and he's fabulous. He listens to me and if he thinks it's appropriate, he'll take the advice or not and explain why. It's a good collaborative effort.

"I actually thought this was a great opportunity, because everything is acceptable for the character. I knew this would be a great place to get my chops wet because the character is limitless. Nikita has to constantly adjust to new situations and never forget that the people she works for are killers. Sometimes she completely denies that they are, just to get through it, but it's often like treading on glass. I think she'll never believe the Section is a great thing. She understands that her work is important, but at the same time although their ends are just, their means are ruthless. The only way to beat these guys is to join them and be better than them at what they do. *Then* you can get them. So it's all about her tak-ing information now and covering the fact that she's never going to be like them, while letting them think she's becoming the spy they want her to be. It's always up her sleeve that she's not and one day she'll spring and get them, or have them at *her* mercy. It's kind of like she's biding her time, like a panther. Waiting. Watching them. Studying them."

Two things that do *not* influence her performance, she emphasizes, are the original 1990 French film or the 1993 American remake starring Bridget Fonda, *Point of No Return.*

"I saw the French film when it first came out years ago and loved it," she smiles. "I sat there and said, 'I can do that.' When I got the show and went in for the audition, my manager said, 'You *are* this role, just go in and have fun.' So I sort of went in, tore up offices and did all kinds of things and just had a great time. Nikita has changed a lot from the feature, because it's for television and you have to turn it down and tame it down. In the first few episodes I was full on, right out there and the executives were a little nervous, so I pulled it back a bit. So I really didn't need to see the movies to find out who she was. I sort of approached it as I would any character in any play, and probably did way too much work. But it helps in that my mind is full of the character's thoughts.

"I think each actor has a different interpretation of any role," she continued. "If, for example, I played Martha in *Who's Afraid of Virginia Woolf?*, it would be very wrong of me to look at Elizabeth Taylor's performance and then say, 'Well, how did she do that?' and work it out and then create the character. It's the same thing with Nikita. If I

had looked and studied the film, I would be all screwed up. The truth is, to play a character well and right, to play the human being, you have to go down inside your own heart. And the only way you do that is through the technique of understanding how to break down a character technically. You find the answers within the text and within yourself. And so the Nikita I created is completely my own, and she reacts the way that she does in the show and it's very different from the film. In some ways the pilot was similar to the film with some good adjustments. What an interesting role for a

DON FRANCKS (WALTER)

As Q is to James Bond, Walter is to Section One, the oldest member of Section, and the man who comes up with many of the team's high-tech gadgets.

Born and raised in Vancouver, Don Francks made his acting debut at age eleven onstage in *The Willow Pattern Plate*. This veteran performer's varied television credits include *Jericho, Drying Up the Streets, The Phoenix Team, Top Cops, Mister Rogers, Road to Avonlea, Ice Princess, The Wild Wild West, The Man From U.N.C.L.E.*, and *Mission: Impossible*. He has been seen on the big screen in such features as *Finian's Rainbow, Fast Company, My Bloody Valentine, Married to It*, and *Johnny Mnemonic*. He has also provided voice-overs for numerous commercials and animated series, including *Beetlejuice, Free Willy, Cadillacs & Dinosaurs*, and *Inspector Gadget*. Additional stage credits are *The Flip Side, On a Clear Day You Can See Forever, Kelly*, and *Leonard Bernstein's Theatre Songs*.

woman. As a film role for women, I think *Nikita* will go down as a really interesting role, whether I played it or not. So I think I've made her my own. You can't do anything and try to copy somebody else. I tend to flip over the rock. She wants to get to what's underneath, and as an actress I like to do that, too."

One of the most common questions Wilson has been faced with concerns the similarities and differences between her own self and her on-screen alter ego.

"It's so bizarre, but how Nikita feels about the Section is generally how I feel about Hollywood," she says. "Not that I dislike Hollywood, but I'm from something so foreign and I'm acting because I love it and I have a lot of energy. And it's not an

Albert L. Ortega

La Femme Nikita has transformed Peta Wilson from struggling actress to superstar and cult figure.

ego trip for me or having to assert my identity. It's just because I really like doing it and I love telling the truth and love that I have the ability to be like a window and tell the truth about people that I play. I can actually get my ego out of the way and do that very well. So for me, the metaphor's humongous. I guess I just don't like people telling me that something can't be done. And they're in the position of power, that they can say yes or no, and things happen. But they don't even try because they can't be bothered. That gives me . . . a real pepper up my butt. And I always look for a way around people like that. 'There's a reason he's like that. He wasn't loved. He needs love.' So what we do is smother them in love. Kind of like a bee with honey. Give them enough, they'll drown themselves. So it's kind of like that in *Nikita*. Even in these really, really bad people. She's always looking for that, a reason why they're doing it, so that maybe she can give them what they need.

JOEL SURNOW (EXECUTIVE CONSULTANT)

A UCLA Film School graduate, *La Femme Nikita* guiding force Joel Surnow first began his writing career by penning episodes of *St. Elsewhere.* His first big break was as executive producer of NBC's ultra-glitzy *Miami Vice* in the 1980s.

"I got hooked into *Miami Vice,* where I became head writer the first season and literally wrote almost all of that show," Surnow explained. "There was no writing staff because Michael Mann kept firing everybody." He then shifted over to the Edward Woodard series, *The Equalizer,* before taking up the prime-time soap opera *Falcon Crest,* where he was given creative carte blanche over the struggling series.

"We did the best season of television ever produced," he smiles. "We outdid *Twin Peaks* with the crazy stuff we did. It wasn't as obscure as *Twin Peaks,* but it was really a wild season."

Tweaking soap-opera conventions was fun, but it wasn't what Surnow had in mind for a career. So after a stint on the short-lived TV version of *Bill and Ted's Excellent Adventure, Covington Cross,* and *The Commish,* he became supervising producer of *Nowhere Man.* That UPN series, which chronicled the adventures of photographer Thomas Veil (Bruce Greenwood), whose existence had been "erased" by an all-encompassing conspiracy, got off to an impressive start, garnering solid ratings as well as critical kudos

"Could I do what she does? If my child's life was in danger, I'd be gone. If I had to defend myself, I would defend myself as best I could. But I would never want to kill somebody. Just to have Nikita do it is hard enough. But love one another, right? Killing is not cool. I'd try to talk my way out of it. If all else failed, I'd try to hurt him or her. Nikita was like I was seven or eight years ago. She's so innocent. And she has a certain naïveté that is very warm. She has a naïveté in this modern world and the world that she's from. She has a vulnerability, like an animal. Like an innocent animal."

Wilson probably isn't as innocent as she once was, given the huge success of the show and the fact that she seems to be *everywhere*—from magazine covers to numerous television appearances, among them *The Tonight Show* and *The*

JOEL SURNOW, continued

for its innovative twist on the paranoia trend that flourished in the wake of *The X-Files*. But the show saw its ratings decline and was canceled after its first season. If nothing else, the frustrating experience made Surnow realize that he wanted to tackle series development himself.

"*Nowhere Man* grew to piss me off," he says. "Honestly, I don't know if there was enough on the concept to do twenty-five episodes. I felt like we should have done a couple of episodes à la *The Prisoner,* then we'd move into a *Three Days of the Condor* government conspiracy kind of thing. But that's not what we did—we just stayed with the initial premise, which doesn't suggest a ton of material. I think there's a reason a show like *The Prisoner* only ran for seventeen episodes—I'm sure they ran out of ways to jerk the audience around. *Nowhere Man* was like that—it had nowhere to go. [Series creator] Larry Hertzog looked at the show as *The Prisoner,* he didn't think it needed to go anywhere. He just wanted to be allegorical and didn't feel that they needed to have a linear progression. As a result, the show was limited."

And after a brief stopover as writer and executive producer of the *Wiseguy* reunion movie, Surnow moved on to *La Femme Nikita,* which he feels puts him in control of his creative destiny. "You basically have to reinvent yourself in this business sometimes, which I did. Now I am on *Nikita,* doing a good one-hour action show. It feels really great."

Rosie O'Donnell Show. "I feel like I'm a saleswoman," she says. "We've got this huge conglomerate. It's like a big building and everyone else is working on it. Without the tiler, the painter, the plumber—we have no building. But guess what? I'm the saleswoman, so they build the whole thing and make it look really great. And I get out there, and I'm the one who sells it. The truth is, I embrace my crew and love them, so I share the whole experience with them. If given the opportunity, I'd say thank you to my crew. Because without them, *La Femme Nikita* wouldn't be. I'm grateful and gracious to the fans because without them, I wouldn't be employed again this year. They take the time to watch the show, and it's nice because I work really hard to make the show. I'd never really done a series and I wasn't really expecting anything."

The loss of privacy is also something new she has begun to deal with. "Mum and I were in New York a couple of weekends ago," she said to Rosie O'Donnell. "We went out for a couple of quiet drinks, a little bit of dinner. There were a lot of people that came up and recognized me. It was very nice, just a bit strange. And Mum said, 'You don't get very much privacy, do you?' No one knows who I am down there [Australia]. Which is kinda great. I just bought ten acres of land on the most *beautiful* beachfront in OZ, where I went camping with the family last Christmas. It was a real, kinda low-down Australian Christmas. And we had trailers and you had to wash your feet in buckets before you got in bed. There's nothing like sand in the bed."

Relishing this newfound success, Wilson also looks to the future, contemplating where her career might take her one day. "My favorite actors are Gena Rolands and Jessica Lange," she says. "I thought Natalie Wood was good in *This Property is Condemned*. I like Tennessee Williams and the women in his plays. I like to do comedy. I want to do very honest roles, and I feel like I'm an actress who will try, or do, anything. I like to play women who are very interesting. I don't see myself in conventional roles. I don't think people will buy that. I'm developing scripts with my production company.

One character is an alcoholic who stuffs mattresses for a living, drives around in a Pinto, and listens to Sonic Youth. Good scripts are good. We'll see what comes to me, what I get."

The actress has also given a lot of thought to her alter ego, Nikita, developing not only a past for the character—which the audience will never actually see—but thoughts concerning a possible direction for her.

"I think basically she's a victim of circumstance," Wilson states. "She didn't have a great childhood. She was moved around a lot. Her mother sort of fell in love with the big guy at school and got pregnant, and he sort of washed his hands of her. In some ways, I think Nikita kind of ruined her mother's life just by way of her birth. Nikita was shipped around to relatives and stuff until the mother decided she wanted to come and try out being with her. It sort of became that Nikita was more the mother than the mother was

> **" My hat comes off to USA for taking a risk with me—a complete unknown actress who had very little experience on camera, and for the show itself. I'm pleasantly surprised. "** —Peta Wilson

in the relationship. The mother sank into alcoholism and all kinds of things. Nikita was never really loved by her mom, and was the bane of her mother's existence. It killed Nikita, and she did everything she could to try and get the love she needed from her mom or have a role model. It's very sad, really, because I think in the end her mother forced her to go and live in the street by always bringing her boyfriends back to the house, and these boyfriends were abusive to Nikita.

"I think that's where Nikita became very spontaneous in defending herself," she elaborates, "because I think she had to fend off these weird, strange, horrible men that her mother would bring back. She was forced to

> **"** [Peta] was also guided by her family's mobility, preventing development of long-term relationships, which meant she had to adapt quickly, sizing up social situations and doing whatever would help her rapidly fit in. Ironically, it was the perfect training ground for essaying the role of Nikita. **"**

live on the street, and I think that's interesting because there are a lot of kids on the streets who aren't drug addicts, who are basically victims of circumstances, who aren't loved or wanted, so they're forced out. That's what Nikita is. Not a drug addict [or] a bad person, just someone who was unloved. Because of being unloved it builds a lot of character traits that are defensive and defiant and sensitive. Of course she's got to protect herself if she's going to live on the street, so that would really toughen you up. In the course of that,

sort of drifting around the place, looking for where she should fit. She would go back to see her mum or would watch from a distance.

"What happened," Wilson adds to the scenario, barely hiding her enthusiasm, "is, one night Nikita was watching her mother's apartment building, sort of pining, and the boyfriend at the time came back and saw the mother dancing, drinking wine and dancing, which Nikita was enjoying watching, [when] the boyfriend sort of ran up the steps and started laying into her. Nikita comes up the steps, starts laying into him to save her mother, thinking, *This is the way,* and her mother sort of told her to get lost [and] how could you do this? And this was sort of the deciding factor for Nikita that *This isn't it.* Of course, when they showed a picture of her funeral and her mother didn't come, it reiterates that the woman didn't give a shit about her. Living on the street, I think Nikita slept up-top above the world, where it would be kind of safer. She took odd jobs to get herself by and survive. Sometimes she would steal food. I don't think she would steal money, particularly, unless of course . . . she *was* a hustler, she'd hustle in pool halls and stuff. This is all in my head. She was sort of a hustler, and would always collect old pairs of sunglasses she would find, and these became part of her . . . when she was deciding today what kind of character she would be in order to hustle the money she needed, her chameleonness would come out. She had no role model and didn't know who she really was, so it was constantly changing as she was trying to find out who she was and where she should be. She didn't really fit into any group. She was very attracted to animals, especially animals in a zoo—these wild, untamed, beautiful animals who had the spirit beaten out of them, which is a bit like Nikita in the Section.

"The night she was found guilty, [pilot episode] she was hanging out on the street with a girlfriend of hers, another street kid. She started walking to the place she sleeps. On her way down her alley she hears this noise, and there it is: this cop being stabbed to death by this weird guy. Nikita is just shocked and has to fend him off. Nikita is not a killer, but she will defend herself to death. That's what happens, she was defending herself and got caught with a knife, and all of a sudden she's put into this weird world, kind of like the Addams Family and being mistaken because . . . you know when the world sees people: 'Look where he lives, look how he or she looks, they're bad people.' You can't judge a book by its cover, and in the Section's case, they did judge me by the way I looked, not even thinking about what the truth might be.

"They think Nikita's an angel in wolf's clothing. I think every time Nikita kills somebody, she turns off. I don't know; if I was a killer, what would I do? What I think will happen in the show is that it will eat her up eventually, she'll get ulcers, she'll get sick, because she's holding on to it. The truth of the matter is that she's never going to be a killer. She has to do it to survive, but it never gets easier. There's an episode in which a friend is killed, and it's kind of like vengeance, in a way, or vigilante, in a way; but that's the only time that it's happened, because she can remember her friend screaming as she died, so this guy should go down. But even so, afterwards you don't feel good about it. That's the thing, she's really no different than anybody else who would be put in the situation.

"A lot of the work that I'm doing, now that I've formed the character, is just working in the moment. I think there's a certain attitude and edge that I have, or a certain way that I perceive the world that isn't unlike Nikita. I'm weary, at times, of people and their humanity, or how they are, or lack of humanity. The defiance is definitely similar to my own. That's a very good question for Joel Surnow. There are similarities, but I couldn't name them because I haven't thought about them. The awkwardness. I'm pretty comfortable in most situations, but my awkwardness when I'm around bad people,

people in my life who my instincts tell me are not good. Nikita is similar in that she's very perceptive about people. Not in the beginning, but as the show has gone on, she's becoming much more like I am, which is [having] an instinctual feeling about people. I think Nikita will give people a chance, but if they blow it . . . that's very similar to me. I always give people second and third chances because I always believe and hope that individuals will grow.

"I think there's also a comfort she has in [her] own sexuality—she's becoming more comfortable and realizing that it is a valuable asset. Not *sex,* but vulnerability and femininity, and that what makes us different from boys is very powerful. Her situation being a spy, she can really manipulate a situation to get what she needs. So she has no problems with that. Myself, . . . I have no problems with that. I don't like it when people are rude or ugly. I hope they see what's past the external. I think the key to her, as well, is that sometimes when she goes into a situation, the guys are really lecherous. It makes her even more: 'I'm going to get this.'

"I love sunglasses, and she loves sunglasses. When she goes out to do a job and she's Nikita the spy, she puts sunglasses on. Nikita is not a very good liar. Not like most killers would be. She wears the sunglasses to hide it until it's done, then she'll take [them] off. Just getting over that first hurdle. Sometimes—coming into the Section—it makes her feel so uncomfortable there. It's so anal and corporate, that it just feels cold. It's like a reverse vampire effect; she puts on the sunglasses because it hurts her. She doesn't even want to be there. Another similarity between me and the character is, I want things to be comfortable; and Nikita tries that as well. When I go into environments like Section One, which are like corporate offices, I feel uncomfortable and want to kind of break something to shake them up. Undo the ties. Nikita also has a Section life and a home life, and she tries to separate the two. As an actress, I've got my working life and my home life, and I'm constantly trying to keep that balance.

"I would love for the audience to see what a plethora of reality the effects of this could have on her. Kind of like Martin Sheen in *Apocalypse Now.* She's stuck, a prisoner at home, everywhere. I'd love to see her watching old movies like *Mildred Pierce,* or old films that are on television with women being bad girls. Getting an idea of what she'll do. She'll completely submerge herself into playing characters when I go in and do these jobs. Then it's not me, I can justify it because I'm somebody else. What happens then is that Section is very happy, and then you see it starting to unravel. The makeup's a little rough, things aren't quite right. Over the course of three episodes you see Nikita fall apart to the point where she actually lets somebody go because she can't do it anymore. He goes to kill her and she has to kill him and she wants to know: 'Why . . . don't you just go? I'm going to die.' She disappears; they can't find her. Five days later Michael finds me in the sewer around the body doing a whole looney-tunes thing. What comes out of that is, 'Hey, I can't hide from it. I'm actually a killer.' Then she becomes like James Bond."

Wilson starts to laugh at her oration and clarifies, "Hey, these are only my ideas of where it could go. A year ago, I was just beginning to enjoy acting and realizing that I'm pretty good at it. It's great to find something and say, 'Hey, this is what I should be doing; this is for me.' Because I never even envisioned that I would be a working actress, I just enjoyed the process so much. It's nice to have a profession where you're acting, which is not telling the truth, but *still* telling the truth. It's a great job to come to work every day and play another human being, and to make it as truthful as possible. That's what's interesting. Plus, whatever direction the show goes, to just be given the break is fantastic. I'm looking forward to really chomping my teeth and learning the technical things that the theater can't teach you. Hopefully, by the time it's done, I'll be ready for the next step."

chapter three

LA GUIDE NIKITA

SEASON ONE

Episode #1: "Nikita"

Written by Cyrus Nowrateh
Directed by Jon Cassar
Guest Starring Bill MacDonald, Anais Granofsky, Ric Reid, Robbie Rox, Kurtys Kidd, James Vezine, Kevin Connelly, Tony Curtis Blondell, and Pierre Trudell

Press Synopsis: Nikita, a girl living on the streets, is sentenced to life in prison for a murder she did not commit. When the government fakes her suicide, Nikita wakes up in Section One, a top-secret agency that plans to train her as an antiterrorist operative—and she must comply in order to stay alive.

Behind the Scenes: In an interview with *Cinescape* magazine, Joel Surnow admitted that he felt a bit hamstrung during production of the pilot episode for the series because it was an absolute necessity to recreate certain scenes from the Luc Besson feature film.

"We were sure we were going to get hits from the critics who would say, 'Yet another remake of this movie,' but we had to do it," Surnow explained. "We had to establish what the premise of the show was. Comparing it to Luc Besson's *La Femme Nikita*, you could say, 'God, they did the kitchen scene so much better than you did. . . .' I just felt like we were stuck. There was a lot of talk of skipping the premise and going into it like six months into her training, but I felt in terms of telling the story, we had to show it. Look, the people who watch TV are probably not the people who go to foreign films, necessarily. I think it was successful in that way."

Interestingly, the pilot was the third episode shot but the first aired. The reason for this is that Surnow wanted the actors to seem comfortable with one another right from the get-go, when the first episode was broadcast.

Episode #2: "Charity"

Written by Robert Cochran
Directed by Kari Skogland
Guest Starring Simon MacCorkindale, Michael Filpowich, Mackenzie Gray, Gerry Mendicino, Wayne Ward, Ian White, Peter Van Ward, Adriana Galic, Stefan Bragren, and Harve Sokoloff

Press Synopsis: Nikita is assigned to get close to a money launderer in order to steal his data files. When she learns about his successful charity for trou-

bled youth, she starts falling in love with him. However, when Section One admits to Nikita that the shelters are a front for a thriving child-slave trade, Nikita's loyalties become divided.

Behind the Scenes: During an online interview, story editor Michael Loceff detailed the writing process for the series, noting that *La Femme Nikita* is "privileged" to have what he considers to be one of the best acting ensembles working in dramatic television. As Loceff explained it, when he's on-set he has conversations with each of the primary actors, while Joel Surnow is in contact with them on a daily basis. Each actor, he said, has a plethora of ideas in terms of where their characters originate and what direction they're headed.

"The actors frequently have questions about the scripts," he noted. "No one is more sensitive to their character's behavior than they, and they approach these scripts with a high degree of professionalism and scrutiny. Often these interactions result in line changes, other times they will walk away with a better understanding of what is on the page. As a writer, I look at where each actor has taken my scenes in the past and use this as a source of new ideas—things I wouldn't have thought of if I hadn't seen Matthew read a Birkoff line in just *that* way, or Alberta make a choice that surprised me and which turned out better than I had envisioned. In this way the actors guide us in writing future scripts, and in making the characters develop in ways that are very much due to the cast we have, and not some abstract characters."

Reportedly, "Charity" taught the production team an important lesson: Even guest characters have to be presented a certain way or they are not effective. Joel Surnow told one online audience member that Simon Mac-Corkindale's character should not have been dressed in ascots, even if, in reality, it was right for such a character. "In our show," he said, "people have to look

> ❝ Interestingly, the pilot was the third episode shot but the first aired. The reason for this was that Surnow wanted the actors to seem comfortable with one another right from the get-go, when the first episode was broadcast. ❞

like Section characters and talk like Section characters, even if they're not in the Section. There's a uniformity in style that eclipses reality. We were a little reality-driven in that show. When you do a stylized show, that's always the hardest thing to grasp."

Genre fans will probably remember guest star Simon MacCorkindale for his starring role in the short-lived NBC science-fiction series, *Manimal.*

Episode #3: "Love"

Written by Michael Loceff
Directed by Jon Cassar
Guest Starring Tobin Bell, Valerie Boyce, James Gallanders, Blaine Joseph Bray, Ryan

Greene, Alisa Wiegers, Marquis Bobesich, Frank Tiefenbach, Marie Cruze, Dominic Fung, and Ho Chow

Press Synopsis: When an international arms smuggler steals a canister of deadly nerve gas, Nikita and Michael pose as a married mercenary couple in order to infiltrate the smuggler's compound. However, when the gas is discovered wired to a bomb in a crowded train station, Nikita must put her life on the line to defuse it.

Behind the Scenes: "Love" was actually the first episode shot and in comparison to the way that the show looks now it is radically different in its approach. First of all, there was a *lot* of action written into the script, as the producers feared a new ensemble cast might not be able to carry the load of the show. It is obvious their fears were unfounded. This group of actors instantly gelled on camera, as though they had been working together for years. Most important, it established an instant rapport between Peta Wilson and Roy Dupuis, whose Nikita and Michael would ultimately become the core of the series.

Joel Surnow has admitted that he had some initial concerns about the way that Dupuis was playing Michael: understating just about everything and allowing his eyes to do the acting. "He's just so calm and so cool," Surnow told *RetroVision Online*. "I started to fight him on that show to convey a little more urgency, because he took everything in such stride. Now I look at it and I realize that he was right. He's not a skittish character, he does everything in his measured doses. In terms of the learning curve, that's where I came out on that."

Episode #4: "Simone"

Written by Michael Loceff
Directed by Jerry Ciccoritti
Guest Starring Mung-Ling Tsui, Julian Richings, and Ingrid Veninger

Press Synopsis: Glass Curtain is a high-tech terrorist organization that attracts new members via Internet chat rooms. Posing as a new recruit,

Nikita is taken to Glass Curtain headquarters, where she discovers that Michael's wife, Simone, is being held hostage. A former Section One operative, Simone was believed killed years before. Now, Michael's continued love for Simone may threaten the success of Section One's attempted infiltration of Glass Curtain.

Behind the Scenes: The primary reason "Simone" was written was to give an answer to fans of *La Femme Nikita* who wanted to know why Michael and Nikita weren't getting together romantically. As Joel Surnow has mused elsewhere, the concern was that the audience might think Michael was gay or something, because it wasn't as though it would have been illegal for them to

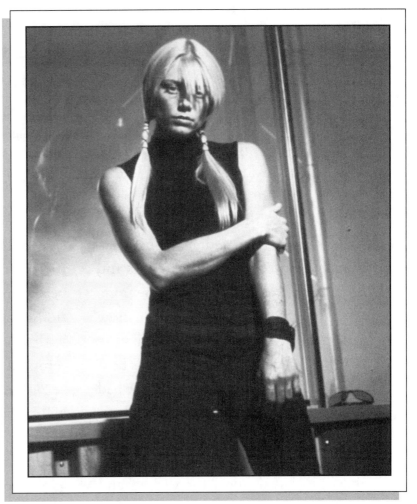

USA Network/Shooting Star

Peta Wilson adds surprising depth to a TV action heroine.

have a relationship. At the same time, events of the episode in some ways brought the duo closer together, though the ending—as is the case at the closing of many an episode—is rife with ambiguity.

Surnow mused to journalists, "I think the reason people tune into our show is for the [unexpected] element that runs through a lot of the episodes, and the fact that we aren't afraid to take the left turn at the end of a show. When I did *The Equalizer,* people wanted to see him kick ass and win. That was the show. It's the same way that people want to see our show *not* be about the good guys beating the bad guys, but that the good guys beat the bad guys and are *worse* than the bad guys. *That's* us."

Another accomplishment of the episode was the fact that by having Nikita do what she does for Michael and Simone, it conveys the depth of her feelings for him. Surnow felt it showcased the complexity of their relationship. "You don't know where it's going," he told journalist Bill Planer. "It's not clean, it doesn't tie up anything. You're just left with a 'feeling,' which our show does when it's working. It's never about closure."

Episode #5: "Friend"

Written by Naomi Janzen
Directed by Guy Magar
Guest Starring Marnie McPhail, David
   Calderisi, Billy Otis, Joseph Scoren, Lorne
   Hunchuck, and Ravinder Toor

Press Synopsis: Section One is assigned to protect Jovan Mijovich, a politician attempting to negotiate peace among opposed forces in his section of the world. When Nikita meets with a contact to find out who has attempted to assassinate Mijovich, she is recognized by Julie, a childhood friend. Nikita attempts to protect Julie's life by creating a new identity for her, but Julie is actually an operative for the organization attempting to assassinate Mijovich.

Behind the Scenes: Despite the fact that each episode has Section One sending agents into various parts of the world to maintain peace or bring down terrorists, the writing staff has been careful to pretty much avoid real-world events.

"*LFN* takes place in a reality which is five degrees to the right and two degrees ahead of the world in which you and I live," Michael Loceff told an online questioner. "We are to the right (or left) of reality in that we don't deal with too many actual locations or incidents in our scripts. We do use the names of some terrorist organizations to help root the episodes in a dash of reality. It is 'ahead' in that it uses a pseudotechnology, which is only partially grounded in reality. This makes it somewhat futuristic. It acknowledges that there are terrorist and antiterrorist activities in both worlds, but a direct connection is never established. In the end, this series is about relationships between people, and we feel that these relationships and the crises that arise out of them are best served by providing a surreal setting."

This being said, Surnow, tongue firmly implanted in cheek, responded on AOL to being asked to consider how Section One would handle dictator Saddam Hussein, "In fact, I've heard that Saddam watches the show to find out about America's counterintelli-

gence. They would kidnap an attaché. Have Madeline torture him until he gave up the location of Saddam. Then Birkoff would run a sim and the team would go out and cancel all seven of him. All seven of 'him' meaning his look-a-likes."

"Friend" was significant to the series in that it was the most organic show that had been offered up until that time. Previously, as Surnow has often conceded, the early episodes had been influenced in tone by the Ken Wahl series *Wiseguy,* and, indeed, there were many similarities. With "Friend," however, *Nikita* moved beyond both the Besson feature and *Wiseguy.* "'Love,' 'Charity' and, to an extent, 'Simone' could have been told on a lot of different shows," Surnow said. "*La Femme Nikita* is the only show where the story of 'Friend' could have been told."

Episode #6: "Treason"

Written by Robert Cochran
Directed by Jerry Ciccoritti

Guest Starring Peter Outerbridge, Vox Flore, Noah Reid, Ted Luczik, Adrian Hough, Tony Neyler, Kim Bourne, Will Corno, and Don Ritchie

Press Synopsis: Section One is assigned by the CIA to "quietly" deport Suba, a foreign antiterrorist contact who is smuggling waste uranium out

FROM NIKITA TO HOMICIDE

"Television writers are like abused children," observed Tom Fontana, the guiding force behind NBC's *Homicide* and HBO's *Oz.* "It's hard for us to accept that anybody likes us."

Well, get used to it, buddy. As motion pictures continue to fill theaters with empty spectacles loaded to the box office with pyrotechnics and one-dimensional characterizations geared toward younger and younger demographics, television has been maturing very nicely, thank you.

The tube is most definitely alive with the sound of drama, in many ways filling a void created by the studios' desire for the next megablockbuster. Move from network to network and you'll find a variety of dramatic series—some lighter than others—that are challenging the imagination of the viewing audience and bringing the medium to places it's never been before. Among them are such distinct efforts as *Law & Order, The X-Files, Chicago Hope, ER, Homicide, NYPD Blue, Ally McBeal, Buffy the Vampire Slayer,* and *The Practice.* Cable offerings include the aforementioned *Oz* and USA's *La Femme Nikita,* while first-run syndication rounds things out with, among others, *Star Trek: Deep Space Nine, Highlander: The Series,* and *Gene Roddenberry's Earth: Final Conflict.*

"One of the ways that movies have changed is that not many people are trying to make thoughtful, provocative films," offers *Law & Order* executive producer Dick Wolf. "It's almost an oxymoron. The great bulk of studio pictures are geared to eighteen- to twenty-four-year-old men, which is not to say that eighteen- to twenty-four-year-old men are idiots, but they do respond to less cerebral entertainment, especially in features. The basis of the movie business now is event pictures, which do not call for a great deal of thinking. The subjects that are covered, for example on *Law & Order,* would be a two-million-dollar weekend, with a thousand prints out there. The stories for the most part are not giant bugs invading earth. The other problem is that a movie is a world that has to begin, exist, and end in 110 minutes. A successful one-hour [TV] show runs for 110 *hours* or more. In 110 hours you can really go a lot deeper with character, with situations, with what makes people tick than with what you can in almost any feature film that is a one-character character study."

of the country for his own profit. The first attempt to capture him goes terribly awry, and Nikita is held responsible. Upon further investigation, Nikita discovers a traitor in the Section—but one who is being manipulated by Suba by holding his son hostage. Nikita must now decide whether to risk the

FROM NIKITA TO HOMICIDE, continued

"With an intelligent television show," adds David Kirschner, executive producer of *Earth: Final Conflict,* "you can develop a character and bring that character through the hills and valleys we all go through in life and have the audience watch as the character lives through those different emotions. It's wonderful because you have a host of characters doing that and then you can explore how they play off of each other."

Joel Surnow, the guiding force behind *Nikita,* believes that television is a true homestead for writers, even more so than features, where the scenarist is damn well near the bottom of the food chain.

"The business of making movies is really director-producer driven," he says. "In television, if you're a good writer you work from season to season, your work gets made, and you have your hand in every aspect of making those words that you write come to life. It's not just writing in a vacuum like in features, where they do whatever they want to do with it. Making it as a feature writer is like trying to make it as a tennis star. The top twenty guys make a living and the rest really have to worry about how they do every time they hit the ball. In film now, it's usually not about the script. It's about concept. It's about ILM [George Lucas's Industrial Light & Magic], it's about a star, it's about big. Is a movie like *Volcano* one that is driving you to see it because of its drama? No, it's jacked-up testosterone for the overseas market.

"Interestingly," continues Surnow, "I think *Nikita* and some of the shows I've been lucky enough to work on, like *Wiseguy,* are more feature premises. The *LA Laws, ER*s, and *NYPD Blue*s are brilliant shows. I love them all, but they're really *TV* shows; they're written for the small screen. Lots of interpersonal relationships, lots of character-driven stories. One of the things we try to do, and sometimes we're more successful than at other times, is that we try to do something more along the lines of feature movies we liked in the past before they got too big. Like *Three Days of the Condor, The French Connection*—they're driven by action, but they've also got a nice mix of character with it and they're sophisticated. The way 'A' movies used to be before they got backed up; where they really pushed the envelope

(continued)

wrath of Section One by rescuing the "traitor's" son.

Behind the Scenes: While *La Femme Nikita* is a pretty humorless show, what few people realize is just how much fun the cast and crew have producing it. In several different online interviews, Peta Wilson has noted, "I'm particularly clumsy, so it's a laugh a minute. In one episode, myself and Roy had to wear wetsuits in the stu-

FROM NIKITA TO HOMICIDE, continued

in terms of extreme characters, heroes and villains. I think what we have between Michael and Nikita is a very adult relationship that we don't oftentimes see on television. It's not your typical snappy chatter. It's dangerous and romantic, which is what a lot of action movies used to be about. Steve McQueen movies and movies of the '70s used to have that quality."

Yessiree, the form that had been considered dead by all accounts just a few years ago is now going through a full-blown renaissance.

Matt Roush, former television critic for *USA Today* and currently working in the same capacity for *TV Guide,* notes, "You get a sense that in the better part of their drama development the networks look for something a bit more original. In sitcoms it's a different animal. Certainly NBC has really brought the notion of cloning themselves to a high or low art, depending on how you look at it, and it really does begin to make TV seem so much more irrelevant. But then on Mondays when they're basically running the same sitcom for two hours, you have the choice of watching either *Alley McBeal* or *Buffy the Vampire Slayer,* both very original, very fun shows that are written by terrific writers. Despite its title, *Buffy* is one of the coolest shows on TV. In certain areas of drama development I think they do realize the value of originality in the product. They do allow people like David Kelley, Tom Fontana, Steven Bochco, David Milch, and these people with very strong voices and points of view to flourish."

For his part, Fontana has a different point of view. "I think television is the most cyclical medium around," he says. "Networks usually will look at something that becomes a hit and try to copy it. Think about a half-hour show about a bunch of guys and girls in their twenties sitting around a coffee shop. When that becomes a hit, there are thousands of them and the schedule becomes saturated with the same kind of show. So people say, 'I don't want to watch another sitcom, let's start watching the dramas.' I think that eventually people will get tired of drama again and we'll get back to bowling shows or something."

dio, pretending to be on a Zodiac boat. I took a tumble and all the camera saw were my two legs and flippers pointing up in the air. Roy actually goofs around a lot. There have been times where I've slipped when running in on a scene. . . . There was also a good one at one in the morning, and we had these weird infrared goggles on in twenty-degree weather. We were running around in the bush with guns. We had to hide behind a tree. I

FROM NIKITA TO HOMICIDE, continued

Yet it's undeniable that, unlike the majority of sitcoms that seem to copy each other, the thriving dramas are substantially different from each other. "That's very true," Fontana concedes. "I feel that Kelley, Carter, Bochco, Wolf, and I are doing totally different work, but we're all still reaching for the high bar. I hadn't really thought of it from that point of view, that they're so different. This is totally off the top of my head, but it might be that most television network executives think they know comedy. None of them think they know drama. Maybe they leave us alone because they're afraid to have an opinion about it. In comedy, when you sit in the bleachers and there's no laugh at a joke, you can have an opinion about it."

Ron Moore, coexecutive producer of *Deep Space Nine,* believes that one aspect of the television medium that clouds people's perception of it is that there is simply so *much* programming between the networks and cable. "Television," he muses, "is this giant maw that must be fed twenty-four hours a day. The more channels there are, the more programming there is. With the rule that 95 percent of everything is crap; that's a *lot* of crap. But there's also a tremendous amount of very good product on television. There are fewer movies coming out of the feature world, and the ones they do they're risking a lot more money on, they're high-budget projects and have a lot riding on each film. They're just playing it safe, and the bigger budget, mainstream action stuff coming out of Hollywood is very pedestrian, and you've seen it a thousand times. You have to really sift around to find the jewels in the feature world. In television, even the most action-oriented shows can't come anywhere near what you can do on a movie budget. So that's not something we're pressured with. They're not trying to get more bang in there. They're saying, 'You can't produce any more bang, do something else.'"

That "something else" is what's appealing to the majority of these shows' producers. They relish the opportunity to delve into thematic material and character relationships in a way that no other medium would allow them, putting their visions on film with very little in the way of interference.

(continued)

couldn't see a thing and ran into Michael—a stiff character—and he knocked another person over. It was like a domino effect because everyone fell.

"Then," she continued, "in the episode 'War' there was a moment when we broke into this song when some guy stuck a gun in his mouth. We broke into a rendition of 'The Flintstones,' but it was, 'The Section . . . We're the Section,' sung to the tune of 'Flintstones.' We did it as a musical, and faced the camera."

Joel Surnow has pointed out that "Treason," like "Friend," dealt with Ni-

FROM NIKITA TO HOMICIDE, continued

Fontana finds both *Homicide*—chronicling the cases of a Maryland homicide team—and *Oz*—an unrelenting prison drama focusing on life on the inside—to be incredibly fulfilling creatively. "Being the executive producer of the show as well as one of the writers," he explains, "I pretty much set the agenda for the kind of stories that we're going to tell. For me, personally, I'm a kid in a candy store. On any given day I can wake up and say, 'You know, I'm really pissed off about capital punishment. Let's do a show about that.' We get to rant and rave, and for the most part get to do it in the way we want to. So it's an extraordinary position to be in from a writer's point of view. And then being a producer, the great thing is that I get to follow it from the initial idea right through the final edit. I'm involved in every aspect of the production so that, as a writer, I see my vision fulfilled. If it isn't fulfilled, it's my own fault—forgetting about censors and network people."

Fontana looks back to his stint on *St. Elsewhere* as the beginning of his opportunities to dig deeper as a writer. "When we did that show," he says, "the whole idea was to develop the characters without making it a soap opera. For me the challenge has always been to take characters from point A to point B and all the way to Z, and base it on the effect that the job they do has on them. That's why the shows I do are more profession-oriented than, say, *Party of Five*, because, to me, I want to see the wear and tear on a human soul based on being a doctor, a homicide detective, a prisoner."

In the case of *Law & Order,* which is actually growing more popular than ever in its ninth season, Wolf feels that the show's success, and the source of his greatest satisfaction, is the fact that the series is considerably more story driven than character driven, which goes a long way in explaining how it has survived continuous cast changes.

kita helping someone and trying to put herself between the Section and someone else. "At that time and place," he said, "that was what we thought our show had to be—acting outside the directive of the Section for her own agenda, which was always to help someone."

Episode #7: "Mother"

Written by Naomi Janzen
Directed by Guy Magar
Guest Starring Sherry Miller, Wayne Best, Kent Stains, Bruce Tubs, David Blacker, Emanuel Mark, and Roy Doucette

FROM NIKITA TO HOMICIDE, continued

"Even though you know the characters," he notes, "the audience knows if you don't see the show in two weeks or two months or two years, if you come back you're going to get a totally satisfactory hour of television where you're not going to have to know who's sleeping with whom, who's having a nervous breakdown; that the story is going to be complete in and of itself in one hour. I think that's very comforting for the audience. If you look at a lot of shows, what happens fifth, sixth, or seventh year is that the storytelling gets into a very predictable rhythm and it's hard to tell the episodes apart. With *Law & Order,* because it's a completely story-driven show, every story is significantly different. It's an anthology of life in New York, in a sense. People think I'm crazy when they ask me how long I think the show can go and I say that as long as the writing stays up there, there's no reason it can't run another fifteen years and beat *Gunsmoke.*"

One of the medium's biggest appeals to Surnow—and it is so incredibly indicative of life in the '90s—is the instant connection that is made with fans of *La Femme Nikita,* as evidenced by the numerous Web sites and newsgroups devoted to the show.

"It keeps you informed of what people like and don't like, and helps you to refine the show in a way," he says. "At the end of our first season we were able to look back at the first twenty-two shows, studying what worked and what didn't. Simply put, it's a twenty-two-episode pilot, in a sense. Now we're able to get leaner and meaner and get to the point in the second season. I think television allows you to have more feedback and a learning curve. Obviously, with a movie it takes a long time to release it because you want to do that curve with test screenings. But even testing isn't quite as accurate because you only have fifty or a hundred people. That can't do the job for you. But when you have millions

(continued)

Press Synopsis: A nuclear trigger is stolen by a cold-blooded terrorist couple responsible for killing an entire team of Section One operatives. In a final attempt to retrieve the trigger, Nikita poses as the couple's long-lost daughter, who was given up for adop-tion years ago. However, this leads to unexpected consequences for both "mother" and "daughter."

Behind the Scenes: Reportedly there were enormous problems in the writing of this particular episode, and it

FROM NIKITA TO HOMICIDE, continued

of people watching the show each week and commenting on it, you can really work to make it a better series.

"One of the things I love about our show is that our characters are constantly in a state of change, and it constantly throws the actors," Surnow elaborates. "It takes them about a year to nail down this kind of stylized, monochromatic characterization and still give it depth. Now we're asking them to do more things that people do and still keep that cool. We're trying to open up Michael and peer into his soul a little bit, and have Nikita grow. Everyone's changing. She's not the same character she was last year; she's grown up and isn't the wild child anymore. She knows what the deal is. It adds a whole new complex level to her relationship with Michael, and it's caused him as an actor to change."

Ron Moore has an interesting perspective on the feature/television equation, having been involved with *Star Trek* for a number of years, and even cowriting the first two *Next Generation* features, *Generations* and *First Contact*. As far as he's concerned, the major plus of television is the fact that it forces a writer to become more character-oriented than many features allow.

"In the *Star Trek* movies you've got two hours and you're delivering a big action-adventure piece to the audience," says Moore. "You have a lot more money and more time, and you can do a lot of things you can't do on a television production budget and schedule. But on television you have an opportunity to develop the characters over a longer period of time over many different episodes, watching the relationships change, playing around with different spins on the characters. You can make it a richer universe and a richer program, that after a year or two you've created a situation where these characters have entire tapestries of lives. In a two-hour movie, unless you're doing sequels, you're delivering that character to the audience for the first time. That's where you find out who they are, and at the same moment you're meeting them, you're involved in some plot."

went through more drafts than any other script of the first season. Due to the fact that the story line was rather thin, the staff felt that there wouldn't be enough to carry a whole episode, and they were grateful for the skills of guest star Sherry Miller.

Undoubtedly the most disturbing moment of the show is when Section operatives beat the hell out of Nikita, hoping to get Miller's character to talk rather than see her "daughter" injured. It's a very powerful piece of film, and even caused USA [Network] to

FROM NIKITA TO HOMICIDE, continued

As much as he enjoys many of the drama series discussed earlier, Moore is, not surprisingly, partial to *DS9*, largely, he insists, because of the diversity of storytelling the show's format allows. "I can do things like a James Bond spoof, westerns, romance, action-adventure pieces; and you do get to do murder mysteries and personal dramas, light romantic shows. There's just a variety of different muscles that, as a writer, you get to work occasionally, which is fun and keeps it engaging. It's not the same thing week after week, like *Murder, She Wrote*. I would have blown my head out after about a year if I had to come up with a murder mystery every single week. If you have to do one a season, then that's great."

Wolf looks to ABC's *The Practice,* which until recently had aired on Saturday nights at ten before moving to Monday, and actually began to find an audience. He admits to being impressed with the show's ratings progress, and feels that it's indicative of the power of today's dramas.

"*The Practice* sort of beat the crap out of NBC, which was coasting along with the Thrillogy, thinking that was going to be a Saturday staple," he says. "Well, look what happened. A good show came in and captured a segment of the audience that nobody thought was even out there. Hour dramas are back and they're back to such a degree that nobody ever expected, including me.

"They talk about the Golden Age of Television," he closes, "and if you chart the course out over a twenty-year period, usually the dramas include *Naked City, NYPD Blue,* and *Playhouse 90,* which were never on concurrently. In the good old days you had one great drama on at a time. Now there aren't even enough slates for Emmy nominations for shows that in most eras not only would have been nominated but would have won. In my mind, *this* is the Golden Age of Television."

An edited version of this article appeared in Cinescape *magazine. The original extended text appears here with permission of its author.*

debate whether or not the show had gone too far. In terms of the series itself, it proved without question that Section One would go as far as it had to to achieve its goals—even at the expense of thc lives of its operatives. For the writing staff, as Surnow said online, "At the time it was a liberation for us. The network was a little challenged by it, but it became, in a sense, a defining moment in terms of what we could do on this show. It started to show us that anything goes, that the old rules have sort of been discarded and that we were going to go places on this show that we haven't seen other shows go."

Episode #8: "Escape"

Written by Andrew Dettman and Daniel Truly
Directed by George Bloomfield
Guest Starring Jaimz Woolvett, Anais Granofsky, Domenic Cuzzocrea, Philip Williams, Barbara Radecki, Austin Di Iulio, Panou Mowling, Nif, and George Santino

Press Synopsis: A mysterious Section One operative offers Nikita a seemingly ironclad opportunity to escape from Section One for good. All the information he gives her checks out, and Nikita seriously weighs his offer. However, Michael starts making romantic overtures toward Nikita, and her emotions are divided. Is the Section just toying with her to test her loyalty, or is the opportunity to escape a real one?

Behind the Scenes: In an AOL chat, Peta Wilson admitted that this episode was one that had an impact on her. "Look at the stuff they subject me to. Emotionally, the truth is, if my character doesn't go there and I don't make it believable, then the audience isn't going to buy it. So sometimes I have to go to strange places to pull myself to make it real. There's no rehearsal. Only a little prep at night. I get very little sleep, maybe six hours every night. I think 'Mercy' got to me. [And] 'Escape' was a rough one because it was such a metaphor for how I was feeling at the time," she said. "Not having anything outside of the series as a life. Very pent up. It's very bizarre—many times I'm in synch with the character. It will affect my mood. The makeup artists will tell me a week later, saying that I was really out there or was not feeling well. That means I took on the character's state of mind. Working that quickly as an actor, you have to be very emotionally open. I also don't like having to shoot people. Nikita doesn't like it. It doesn't feel very nice."

"Escape" also showcased Michael's ability to manipulate Nikita, raising the possibility that he might have feelings for her so that she'll stay, and then, once she's stuck again, essentially letting her know that it could have all been a lie. "But the thing that Dupuis does that's so amazing is that we write him like he manipulated her," Joel Surnow said in an interview with Bill Planer, "but he plays it with his looks as if he's heartbroken that he had to manipulate her. It just adds that one other level to it that makes it really cook."

Episode #9: "Gray"

Written by Robert Cochran
Directed by Ken Girotti

Guest Starring Callum Keith Rennie, James Widmie, David Jansen, Carlo Rota, Wayne Davis, and Anthony Lenke

Press Synopsis: Section One's computer security is breached and the directory of all their agents is stolen. Michael goes to Prague to reclaim the directory, but the man who stole it is killed by another terrorist seeking the directory for himself. Nikita discovers that it was randomly left with a civilian passenger on a Prague city bus, architect Gray Wellman. Nikita is assigned to Gray in order to get close to him and retrieve the directory, but when she starts falling for him, her actions not only threaten the mission but Section One's very existence.

Behind the Scenes: One question the staff of *La Femme Nikita* has often been asked is how the scripts for the show are brought together. During an online chat, story editor Michael Loceff detailed the process, noting that it involves the staff "cloistering" into an office for days at a time. Ideas are thrown back and forth and eventually a story

Michael (Roy Dupuis) and
Nikita (Peta Wilson):
sexual tension personified.

which necessitates starting back at the beginning.

"Once a story line is established," he explained, "we will assign it to an in-house or freelance writer, based on workload, individual strengths, or preference. After the first draft of the script is handed in, the staff reconvenes and gives notes to the writer for a rewrite or polish. Usually the first rewrite of any script is extensive. In any case, one of the in-house teams—or two working as a pair—will take a final pass at it, scene by scene, until we feel it is 'correct.'"

At that point, the script is sent out to the studio and the network so that the powers that be at both can respond with notes of their own, which will result in additional rewrites. Then it goes to line producer Jamie Paul Rock, who might

emerges. Other times, despite an incredible number of hours devoted to the effort, said story line will not sustain itself for four acts, they discover, tell the writers that the script is impossible to shoot—from a financial standpoint—as written, resulting in still more rewrites. "Even then," Loceff said, "it seems to be unproducible, given the budget. But Jamie and Rocco Mateo, our production designer, work magic and somehow do it all within or under budget and make it look like it cost twice as much. After it is produced and the director has submitted an initial cut, one of us sits with the editor and cuts the show into its final form."

Man, nothin's as easy as it seems.

Episode #10: "Choice"

Written by Michael Loceff
Directed by George Bloomfield
Guest Starring Callum Keith Rennie

Press Synopsis:　The CIA believes that a rogue element of their agency is responsible for a recent massacre of heroin dealers, performed to steal money and drugs as part of an embezzlement scheme. Section One is brought in to clean the house quietly, but Nikita's continued involvement with architect Gray Wellman is hampering her ability to be a reliable operative. As Section One's operation reaches a fevered pitch, Nikita is unable to balance both sides of her life and is forced to make a choice between the organization that controls her life and the one man that she's ever loved.

Behind the Scenes:　"Choice" is one of the few episodes of *La Femme Nikita* since the pilot to utilize significant elements from Luc Besson's feature film. In this case, it's the moment in Venice where Nikita is with her lover and she receives a phone call instructing her to assassinate a target across the street from where she is, taking aim from her bathroom window. The boyfriend in question is Gray Wellman (returning from the episode "Gray"). Joel Surnow considered it significant in terms of the "legend" of the character. "I thought it was important," he told *Cinescape,* "to put her with a boyfriend and have her try to have a real life, and we see how the Section interferes. I guess I also feel her chemistry with Roy is so strong that I never quite believed that she would choose this guy over Roy. Not that she has the choice of Roy."

Why, he mused, would someone like Nikita settle for Gray when Michael is there, even peripherally? It becomes a problematic situation because Michael truly is the guy for her. "Everyone else," he said, "gives the impression that she's just settling. And you don't like to see a main character just settle. I even felt that in the movie."

Episode #11: "Rescue"

Written by Peter Bellwood
Directed by Ken Girotti
Guest Starring Nancy Beatty, Nigel Bennett, Diego Matamoros, Waneta Storms, and Slavko Ilochevar

Press Synopsis: Section One has successfully destroyed a chemical-weapons plant in a former Soviet bloc country, but in the process Michael is wounded and left behind. On the run, he hides in the house of nurse Angie Georgiev. To rescue Michael, Nikita and Madeline pose as cosmetics saleswomen in order to enter the country. Once there, Madeline induces a heart attack in order to be admitted to the hospital where they think Michael is. But when Madeline's cover is blown by a high-ranking military official, Michael must convince Angie to risk everything to help them escape.

Behind the Scenes: Joel Surnow told *Cinescape* magazine that "Rescue" was one of his favorite episodes of the show's first season, mostly because it was a straight-out action show with a lot of movement and very little dialogue used to tell the story. "That's sort of what I pride myself on, if anything, in terms of television," he said. "My favorite movie of all time is *The French Connection*. There's like no dialogue in that movie. You go through it, yet everybody is defined. It's clear who the characters are, and you know what's going on. It's just character through action."

Elsewhere, director Ken Girotti noted that conceptually they walked the line between the present day and a view of postwar Europe, and they went for an Eastern-bloc feel. "Really a Michael episode," he mused, "and it really showed a side of Michael that doesn't often get seen: his compassionate side. He was thrust into an intense relationship with this woman for an extended period of time until he got himself together, and they sort of had to develop a trust for each other. Her dreams of bigger and better things for her life and getting out of the rut that her life was in this country, and his just trying to get out of there. And in the end she saves his life."

Probably the most startling moment in the episode is when Madeline induces in herself a heart attack. Nikita's shock is the same as the audience's: What *is* it with these people?

Episode #12: "Innocent"

Written by Michael Loceff
Directed by George Bloomfield

> **Despite the fact that each episode has Section One sending agents into various parts of the world to maintain peace or bring down terrorists, the writing staff has been careful to pretty much avoid real-world events.**

Guest Starring Maury Chaykin, John Evans, Doru Bandol, Traci Miller, Darlene Cooke, Derek Keurvosk, Michael J. Reynolds, and Lindsay Collins

Press Synopsis: A terrorist group smuggles a live nuclear device onto North American soil and threatens to detonate it in a major city. However, the bomb transfer was accidentally witnessed by Rudy, a simple pizza deliveryman. Section One interrogates him, thinking he was involved, but Nikita believes Rudy's story—that he was in the wrong place at the wrong time. Nevertheless, he will be canceled—unless Nikita can demonstrate that without Rudy's help, the bomb will not be deactivated.

Behind the Scenes: Of this episode, story editor Michael Loceff noted on-line, "The first draft of 'Innocent' was very much like the final. It had a few scenes that needed to be cut for production sake, and other minor changes were made, but in the end it turned out to be one of the scripts whose first draft hit fairly close to the target. Interestingly, the original story line called for more of a streetwise troublemaker. The moment I started in on the teaser, however, I hit on the idea of a rather simple—but 'wise'—pizza driver, and the rest of the script came into focus very quickly. That was a fun script to write. I was very pleased with how it turned out. Our guest star, Maury Chakin, interpreted Rudy brilliantly. On the other hand, I was a little disappointed in the first-act action, before we meet Rudy. The towing of the jet and process shots of the warhead being off-loaded were void of emotional content and I should have worked in more character during that sequence to get to the real story sooner."

There was some debate over the conclusion of the episode, and whether or not Rudy should be canceled. Ultimately, Joel Surnow, who noted in an interview that he is not a "mean" guy or writer, decided that Rudy should live, although he was surprised to see how negatively the show's core fan base reacted to this violation in Section policy. "That told us something about our fans," he said, "which was that they liked how hard and dark we were playing the show and how laser ruthless the Section was."

Episode #13: "Gambit"

Written by Michael Loceff
Directed by Jon Cassar
Guest Starring Harris Yulin, Lindsey Connell,
   Todd William Schroeder, Allan Murley,
   John Ho, Toma Bates, Barbara Stein,
   Lisa Richardson, and Hamish Robertson

Press Synopsis: When Section One attempts to thwart the thief of a canister of Cobalt 60, they lose the Cobalt but capture one of the world's most fearsome terrorists, Gregor Kessler. To find the Cobalt 60, Madeline must interrogate Kessler, who successfully uses his knowledge of Madeline against her. She manages to gain the upper hand by confronting Kessler with the daughter he never met, but when he kills her in cold blood and escapes, Madeline must put her life on the line and confront him alone.

Behind the Scenes: Prior to "Gambit," much of the first season of *La Femme Nikita* was devoted to Nikita's struggle to get her life back, with secondary explorations devoted to the character of Michael. This episode was the start of a concerted effort to add a little bit of flesh and blood to the other characters, thus preventing their aloofness from going from cool and hip to clichéd.

As USA Network President Rod Perth noted in the middle of season one, "I think the show has to retain its essential kind-of-cool attitude, but it has to also be accessible to a broad audience. It can't be *so* cool, like a piece of Miles Davis music, which would result in a very limited audience. It has to be broader than that."

Obviously, the first character to get this "treatment" was Madeline, who in all the previous shows seemed completely unflappable. *Nothing* seemed to get to her. In this instance, though, she was thrown off balance in a stunning verbal spar with Kessler (and anyone impressed with guest star Harris Yulen in this episode, should check out his equally effective performance in the *Star Trek: Deep Space Nine* episode "Duet." In that show he and Nana Visitor—Major Kira Nerys—do the verbal tango).

Episode #14: "Recruit"

Written by Larry Raskin
Directed by Reza Badiyi
Guest Starring Felicity Waterman, Ted Whittall, Greg Campbell, Brian Smegal, and Ron Kashin

Press Synopsis: Nikita is assigned to evaluate Karyn, who is coming to the end of her two-year training period. On a mission to capture a terrorist gone awry, Karyn kills her trainer in cold blood, then lies about it. When Nikita confronts her, Karyn confides that her trainer had repeatedly raped her. This, coupled with the fact that everyone in Section One seems to like Karyn, makes Nikita's decision all the more difficult. But Nikita's feelings aren't good, and she tries to discover the real story about Karyn.

Behind the Scenes: In many ways, "Recruit" was significant because it marked a turning point for the character of Nikita. In essence, she had proven herself as a rookie to Section One and was now ready to move up to the next level, bringing in people beneath her and having to make cold-blooded decisions about them. Indeed, it was a means by which she would prove that she would be able to survive life in Section.

Guest star Felicity Waterman actually came in second place to Peta Wilson during auditions for the role of Nikita. Reportedly Joel Surnow had told her back in the beginning that although she wasn't chosen for the lead they did like her and would use her on the show.

Episode #15: "Obsessed"

Written by Robert Cochran
Directed by T.J. Scott

Guest Starring Yvonne Scio, Douglas O'Keefe, Kelly Fiddick, Tony Chang, and Brian Majenic

Press Synopsis: David Fanning is one of the world's most dangerous hit men, and Section One is powerless to stop him. Fanning possesses "The Book," a collection of top secret information damaging to Western governments; and if the Section makes any attempt on Fanning's life, the book will be released automatically. When the Section's only way in is through Fanning's abused girlfriend, Nikita and Michael are forced to use any means possible to secure her loyalties, although her emotional instability could prove fatal to both of them.

Behind the Scenes: Director T. J. Scott, who recently helmed his first feature film, the forthcoming *Legacy*, starring David Hasselhoff, was at the helm for this episode and described online his experience. "I was able to do what I wanted with the episodes as far as creating a little bit of a different look and feel for each one that I did," he explained. "They didn't hold me back, they let it be edgy, they let it be a little bit European. It has a European feel to it in terms of Rocco Mateo's art direction. It's a little bit retro but also into the future. The reference point[s] we used when they were creating the sets and costumes [were] France and London. What's hip in Europe right now? What's going on over there? Let's see what the Europeans are doing and bring it into the show. What they did differently from the movie is that you don't know where Section is. You think you're in North America, so here's this sort of retro and hip European feel in North America, and it really throws you off balance and you don't know where you are.

"We set up this real cold, high-end, wife-beating hit man named Fanning, played by Doug O'Keefe. Nikita bypasses the security team by posing as fitness trainer to his wife. Meanwhile, Michael is seducing his wife and gets incriminating information from her. The episode deals head on with mental and physical spousal abuse, in a really ballsy way. We showed the abuse; we feel for the woman through Nikita, but then she stands by and watches. The Section uses the abuse to their advantage by working Michael in. Michael comes off as this cold, manipulative kind of guy, and it's tough having your star do that. The characters on that show, including the guest stars, really get into the parts. Because the writers have given them so much to bite into, so much true stuff, they seem to really—more than any other show I've been on—jump in and say, 'I've got the meat here to play with, I'm going to bite in and play a role here.' [In] one of the abusing scenes between Doug O'Keefe and Yvonne, the performance was so riveting and believable when we watched it, we as the crew members got totally caught up in it and we thought that we'd really seen almost the real thing. We called cut and took five before we moved on to the next setup.

"The technique I used in that episode, knowing that's what we wanted, we went handheld on a lot of it. We tried to keep it real edgy and off-kilter and really feeling like you've never got your feet firmly on the

> **"** It started to show us that anything goes, that the old rules have sort of been discarded and that we were going to go places on this show that we haven't seen other shows go. **"**
>
> —Executive consultant Joel Surnow

Part of the intent of this episode was to expand Michael's ability to be a leading man with other women. As Joel Surnow told *Cinescape,* "It exploited two things: Roy's sex appeal and his ability to really attract women who watch the show; and it showed how ruthless he is in terms of Section One. We had T. J. Scott direct that one, and he's got a stunning eye. He gave us a show that looked more *Miami Vice* than the episodes at that time. We had been getting more down and dirty and gray and grim. We shot this episode when spring was breaking out, so there was like an explosion of color."

ground throughout the entire episode. In an episode like that, the characters are off balance, too, because Nikita just wanted to do something and couldn't. I always tend to direct an episode from one of the character's point of view. We sort of take what they're feeling and use that in the camera techniques. So really it was coming from Nikita. She's off balance. This is getting to her so much, the fact that this woman is being abused in front of her. And the camera just pulls away and makes the camera just shrink, too, because Nikita has to pull away from it to preserve her own sanity, otherwise she may go insane just watching this."

Episode #16: "Missing"

Written by Naomi Janzen
Directed by Reza Baidyi
Guest Starring Christopher Kennedy, Dan Pawlick, Tony Nappo, Pedro Salvin, Frederick Broson, and Leanne Adachi

Press Synopsis: One of the members of a criminal organization that steals classified information to sell to the highest bidder is Operations' long-lost son, Steven. Section One's mission is to eradicate this group along with a dangerous terrorist that plans to buy a smart missile chip from them; but Operations asks Nikita to keep Steven alive at all costs. Nikita agrees, only if Operations will let her finally leave the Section for good. He agrees, but Nikita threatens to kill Steven if Operations doesn't keep his word. Unfortunately for Nikita, she is unaware of Michael's true role in the mission.

Behind the Scenes: During one of her many online chats, series star Peta Wilson took the time to offer her opinions of her fellow cast members. "They're fantastic," she enthused. "They're very giving, they're very different, all of them. Alberta [Madeline] has been acting for a very, very long time. Most women of that age can seem to be a little insecure about a young leading lady. But Alberta is very secure in herself and she is giving to me and not at all intimidated by everything coming to me. She's always there to give me a helpful word of encouragement. They all realize I work sixty percent more than they do. So they know how tired I get and how hard it is on me, and they're always there to be nurturing. They become my family in a way.

"Roy is beautiful," she continued, "but it's kind of like working with a very different kind of man, because he's completely opposite to me. He's kind of soft and softly spoken. He's French Canadian and I'm Australian. You couldn't get more opposite. I'm used to dealing with a very different kind of man. Roy is sometimes shocked by me and my antics. Matthew's a sweetheart. He's a very good actor. He's done many things. He was in *The English Patient,* he was in *Love and Human Remains.* He's been in many things. And again, they're really great.

"Gene is a sweetheart. I can't stand the character he plays, but he is a lovely, lovely man. And you couldn't get more of a sweetheart. He kind of wafts onto the set with his little

French beret and his cashmere coat. And he's very debonair. And Don is a very interesting man. He's sung with people like Frank Sinatra. He's a great, great jazz singer and he has an incredible band. Between takes Don sings me jazz songs. And if they're having a bit of a rough day or having a bit of a hard time with some kind of suits or people, Don will come by and give my arm a rub. He will then go and break into song about my eyes or something."

Episode #17: "Noise"

Written by Michael Loceff
Directed by T. J. Scott
Guest Starring Richard Waugh, Verslav
*   Krystzan, Jon Wildman, Angela Ward,*
*   Tara Slone, Dwayne Hill, Lindsay*
*   Collins, Paul Noiles, Andriana Galic,*
*   Stefan Brogren, and Harve Sokolof*

Press Synopsis: While on a mission to tag a stockpile of Stinger missiles, the Section van is breached and Birkoff is forced to defend himself for the very first time. Now, his fear of being killed on future missions is interfering with his ability to protect Section operatives. Unless Nikita can help him overcome this fear, Birkoff is in danger of being canceled.

Behind the Scenes: Observed T. J. Scott, "A lot of these episodes are really psychologically strong. In this one, Matthew Ferguson's character is afraid of going outside and we play with his phobia, and the fact that he's developed it by being in the Section so long. He's lost his contact with the outside world and is afraid to go out into it. I guess it was a psychological episode that Stephen really dug into. There were times when we'd be filming, I'd look up and he'd be crying his eyes out. He just got so into this character. I don't know what he was drawing on, but he certainly portrayed to us that his character had the fear of going out there."

In an online interview, Joel Surnow said of this episode, "The premise behind 'Noise' was, 'Let's see where Birkoff lives, what he does, who he is. Establish to a greater degree the sister/

brother relationship Nikita plays in his life."

Episode #18: "Voices"

Written by Maurice Hurley
Directed by David Warry-Smith
Guest Starring Stephen Shellen, Anais
    Granofsky, Oliver Becker, Chris Warren,
    Jim Codrington, Arturo Fresolone,
    Gina Bertoia, Yuval Daniel, and
    Lindsay Collins

Press Synopsis: While working undercover near a Central European consulate, Nikita is confronted by a known serial rapist. Nikita easily subdues the man, leaving him battered and bruised. O'Brien, the police detective on the case, has been pursuing the man for years, and realizes that the rapist's victim was no ordinary woman. With the help of a witness, he manages to break through Nikita's cover story and track her down. Because O'Brien now knows the truth about Nikita, he will have to be canceled, unless Nikita can turn the situation around to her advantage.

Behind the Scenes: A great deal of fan speculation concerning *La Femme Nikita* has surrounded the relationship between Nikita and Michael. In the same way, actors Peta Wilson and Roy Dupuis have been asked to evaluate each other in terms of the real-life person and their on-screen persona. What follows are a couple of excerpts from online interviews with fans:

Q: Roy, what do you enjoy most about working with Peta, and Peta, about Roy?

Roy: Her originality, her energy, her talent, and her beauty.

Peta: His unpredictability, his control. His very balanced sexuality between masculine and feminine. His passion. And I like his hair!

Q: Peta, what does Nikita think is Michael's strength and weakness, and Roy, what does Michael think is Nikita's strength and weakness?

Peta: I'm still trying to figure it out. But I think his strength is his focus, his weakness is his sister.

Roy: Nikita's strength would be . . . she has many. She's very talented in many ways. Which makes her a great operative to be in the Section. She's also very pure in a certain way, very original. Her weakness? Her heart, for sure. A weakness in that reality would be her caring for people, her attachment to people around her.

Episode #19: "War"

Written by Maurice Hurley
Directed by Rene Bonniere
Guest Starring James Faulkner, Costa Ka-
*   materos, Coman Poon, and Christine*
*   Van Haltern*

Press Synopsis: The Section's stolen directory has ended up in the hands of Red Cell, and operatives are being hit around the country. Section is being forced to evacuate. In order to learn Red Cell's next move, Nikita and Michael attempt to capture Red Cell's counterpart to Birkoff, but instead they themselves are captured and tortured. Neither of them are willing to divulge Section's current location, but when Michael admits his love for Nikita, she breaks, because she cannot stand to see Michael tortured any fur-

ther. Far from destroying Section One, Nikita quickly discovers that this was the intended plan all along, and Section has a big surprise for Red Cell.

Behind the Scenes: "War" was actually voted as the number-one episode among the show's fans, as evidenced from a call-in and Internet campaign run by the USA Network when they were planning on rerunning a certain number of episodes. In an interview, Joel Surnow surmised this show was so popular because it was probably the darkest show they had shot.

"It really went into *1984* territory," Surnow stated on *RetroVision Online.* "It really took a lot of the elements of our show to its extreme lengths: underground spaces, dark, devious manipulations of people, Michael and Nikita at the core of it, holding on to each other at the face of imminent death, conveying real feelings for each other only to find out at the end that it's all been a manipulation on Michael's part to control Nikita. It really scored high for us. We dumped every conceivable lump of shit on Nikita last year, and that was sort of the culminating episode for that."

Episode #20: "Verdict"

Written by Robert Cochran
Directed by Gilbert Shilton
Guest Starring Eric Peterson, David Calderisi,
  Kate Greenhouse, John-Patrick Mavric,
  Mary Moore, and Joanna Bacalso

Press Synopsis: Jovan Mijovich has been elected as the premier of his new nation, but there is a hit man out to assassinate him. Nikita and Michael, along with other Section One operatives, are dispatched to provide security. During the inaugural celebration, the hit man is taken out, but a hostage situation develops that no one expected. A man, Bruner, claims Mijovich raped and blinded his daughter during the nation's civil war, and threatens to kill him. Nikita tries to defuse the situation and manages to keep Mijovich alive for the time being. But when Bruner's daughter appears to give her side of the story, the accuracy of her testimony will mean the difference between peace and war for her people.

Behind the Scenes: "Verdict" was *La Femme Nikita*'s take on *Death of a Maiden*, exploring the contradiction that sometimes the people we think are the bad guys turn out to be good, and how in this global scheme of things the Section sometimes ends up protecting bad people rather than the good ones.

Episode #21: "Brainwashed"

Written by Peter Bellwood
Directed by Rene Bonniere
Guest Starring Janet Lo, William Colgate, Steve
  Mousseau, David Dunbar, Fred Lee, Alex
  Stapley, and Connor Devitt

Press Synopsis: When Nikita is sent to investigate a bartender, working in a posh club, who may be a terrorist contact, he responds to her questioning by leaping from the sixty-fifth-floor window to his death. A search of his apartment turns up a strange helmetlike device, which Section later discovers is used for brainwashing. Unfortunately, Nikita has used the device several times in an effort to discover what it is, and now it is in control of her mind. When Nikita and other operatives are assigned to protect the premier of China from other similarly brainwashed individuals, Section has no idea that the greatest threat to the premier is Nikita herself.

Behind the Scenes: In some ways, *La Femme Nikita* came *this* close to entering science-fiction territory with "Brainwashed," the show's take on *The Manchurian Candidate*. At the same time, it was analogous to a story of drug addiction, made extremely tangible by Peta Wilson's portrayal of Nikita's cathartic release of childhood demons.

In its third year, the series could very well continue approaching science-fiction borders, particularly considering, as the staff has often maintained, that *Nikita* is a show set "five minutes in the future." As Joel Surnow has explained, it's not so futuristic that you're talking about people in flying cars but rather about issues such as artificial intelligence, gene splicing, and genetic engineering. In other words, things that are going to be happening in the next century. "That's what 'Brainwashed' did for us," he said. "Look at the multilayered aspects of the show. You have the romance and the Section; and one element that's exploitable for us is technology. What is going on on both sides of the fence in terms of technology, what the bad guys are doing and what the good guys are doing. That's a real promising area for us."

Episode #22: "Mercy"

Written by Michael Loceff
Directed by Joseph L. Scanlan
Guest Starring Sean Whalan, Richard Clarkin, Alan Mozes, Gerry Salsberg, James Kirchner, and Kay Valley

Press Synopsis: While tracking down Tyler, a fearsome terrorist, Section discovers that the employee of one of Tyler's contacts has invented a plastic explosive that is completely undetectable. When Tyler kidnaps the young man, Nikita is given orders to cancel him. She refuses. Operations decides that Nikita has finally crossed the line and he sends her on a suicide mission with other operatives set to be canceled. Without Operations' knowledge, Michael gives Nikita the means to escape, but her freedom will change both of their lives forever.

Behind the Scenes: As season one came to a close, Peta Wilson noted to online fans the type of direction she'd like things to go in the second year. "I'd like her [Nikita] to be a little more like she's got their number," she pointed out. "'I got that number. I've had that happen before.' I'd like to see her dominate more. The only way she's going to get out is to get them. I think she might get real good next year. I just try to take a deep breath and do the things she doesn't want to do. I don't think she'll accept what she does, but it's certainly not something I'm thinking about now. She knows it's the way it is, but she doesn't have

to like it. She's trying to find a way to get out."

Of this episode, she added elsewhere, "It's my favorite episode, because I feel like it's the most honest. I had had to tone my character down a bit throughout the season. The producers and I sort of met each other halfway on some character issues. For me as an actress, the finale was the most fulfilling experience. I really felt Nikita was really in a place that I wanted her to be at and I think we see so much of who she really is in that episode, and everything sort of comes out there."

Joel Surnow highly praised the season-one finale in an online interview, noting that it was an episode that went in myriad directions, yet somehow managed to stay contained. As he explained it, the intent was to tell the story of an innocent man who got in over his head, and Nikita finally coming to her wits' end. "We wanted to reconnect Michael and Nikita and get her out of the Section," he said. "The story kind of traveled to a lot of different places, but it was all part of an organic place. Real successful for us."

SEASON TWO

NOTE: *Due to the fact that at press time La Femme Nikita had barely reached the mid-point of its second season, this portion of the episode guide is designed to provide a bit of plot information. Unlike the season one coverage, it does not go behind the scenes due to the fact that it's unclear where year two's shows will ultimately go.*

Episode #23: "Hard Landing"

Written by Michael Loceff
Directed by Jon Cassar
Guest Starring Earl Pastko, David Nerman, Johnie Chase, Makoto Kabayama, Arthur Eng, Valeri Outcharoy, Louis Wrightman, Patric Masurkevitch, and Rolf Huhn

Press Synopsis: With Michael's help, Nikita survived the destruction of a Freedom League hideout in the first season's final episode. Since then, she has been on the run from Section One. While working as a waitress, Nikita is captured by the Freedom League and used as bait to avenge Section One. During Section's raid, Nikita manages to escape and save Michael's life. Later, on an abandoned ship, she and Michael share a night of passion. However, Michael and Nikita's lie about her true whereabouts is in danger of being exposed.

Episode #24: "Spec Ops"

Written by Robert Cochran
Directed by T. J. Scott
Guest Starring Bruce Payne, Nicu Branzea, and Derwin Jordan

Press Synopsis: Nikita is assigned to a special operative, Jurgen, to be retrained following her capture by the Freedom League. When Section is contacted by Kudrin, a Freedom Leaguer who could verify Nikita's story, Section seeks to capture him for questioning. To keep Kudrin from revealing the truth, Michael deliberately attempts to kill him during the mission, but Kudrin survives, and Madeline as well as Jurgen start unraveling Michael and Nikita's lie.

Episode #25: "Third Person"

Written by Michael Loceff
Directed by Jon Cassar
Guest Starring Bruce Payne, Michaeri, and Darren Andrea

Press Synopsis: Birkoff discovers that a seemingly random series of terrorist activities are being perpetrated by a six-man mercenary army that Section One dubs "Helix." Jurgen helps Nikita back to full operative status in preparation for Section's attack against Helix, but Michael is concerned about Nikita and Jurgen's growing relationship. Convinced Jurgen is manipulating Nikita in order to expose her, Michael and Jurgen come to blows.

Episode #26: "Approaching Zero"

Written by Michael Loceff
Directed by Rene Bonniere
Guest Starring Bruce Payne and Farzad Sadrian

Press Synopsis: Jurgen's freedom within Section One fascinates Nikita, and she continues to spend more time with him, despite Michael's disapproval. Michael warns Nikita that Jurgen is not who he claims to be, but Nikita ignores Michael's advice, and she and Jurgen grow ever closer. Unfortunately, Nikita has become an unwitting pawn in a power struggle between Jurgen and the Section, which could mean deadly consequences for Jurgen . . . and Nikita.

Episode #27: "New Regime"

Written by Robert Cochrane
Directed by Jon Cassar
Guest Starring Nigel Bennett and Dean McDermott

Press Synopsis: A Section operative goes crazy and shoots Operations during a briefing. While Operations is on the verge of death in intensive care, Egran Petrosian—the deep-cover agent rescued last season—takes over Section and promotes Nikita to second in command. Despite warnings from Madeline, Nikita

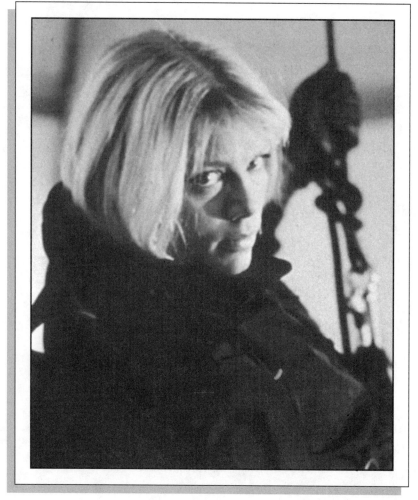

USA Network/Shooting Star

Season two continued the development of Nikita, turning her into a multi-dimensional human being.

Petrosian asks Nikita to murder Operations, the future of Section hangs in the balance.

Episode #28: "Mandatory Refusal"

Written by David Ehrman
Directed by Ken Girotti
Guest Starring Gregory Hlady, Raman Podhara, Christopher Clements, Chantal Quesnel, Kelly Grando, Jake Simmons, Eduardo Gomez, and Allan Chow

Press Synopsis: When Michael is sent to assassinate an arms supplier, the operation is breached and Michael enters "mandatory refusal"—a situation where he must break off communication with Section and complete the mission at all costs. Unfortunately, the arms dealer kidnaps Madeline, and Op-

believes that Petrosian is the better man to run Section One because of his straightforwardness. But when erations believes the only way to protect her is to kill Michael, if necessary. However, Nikita has other plans.

Episode #29: "Darkness Visible"

Written by David Ehrman
Directed by Ken Girotti
Guest Starring Kyle Downes, Kevi Katsuras, Tara Sloane, Damir Andrei, Ned Vukovich, Anna-Louis Richardson, and Andy Rukavina

Press Synopsis: Section One attempts to stop a bombing at a schoolyard, and Nikita observes that Michael knows more about the nature of the bomb than he should. When Nikita questions Michael about this, he brushes her off; but Nikita knows he is hiding something. The next day, she follows Michael and discovers that he is meeting the bomber. Michael and the bomber, Rene, were student protesters involved in terrorist activities in the 1980s, and their paths have crossed once again. But when Operations asks Michael to betray his friend, Michael's loyalties are divided.

Episode #30: "Half Life"

Written by Maurice Hurley
Directed by Rene Bonniere
Guest Starring Denis Forest, Martine Rochon, Genevieve Langlois, and Tannia Burnett

Press Synopsis: Nikita and Michael are sent to a Balkan nation to assassinate Radovan Luka, an arms buyer for rebels who are waging a campaign of ethnic cleansing. When Nikita and Michael arrive in the country, they discover two displaced children, and Nikita forces Michael into protecting them. However, the children's safety distracts Nikita from her opportunity to shoot Luka, and now Nikita and Michael must risk their own and the children's lives by infiltrating a Balkan death camp to kill him.

Episode #31: "First Mission"

Written by Peter Mohan and Jim Henshaw
Directed by Guy Magar
Guest Starring Janet Kidder, Diego Chambers, Peter Mensah, Neno Vojionovic, Peter McDougal, and Amanda da Silva

Press Synopsis: Nikita becomes team leader of a mission for the first time, but her unconventional decisions put her in danger of being canceled.

Episode #32: "Open Heart"

Written by Elliot Stern
Directed by Rene Bonniere
Guest Starring Gina Torres, Jill Dyck, and
    David Collins

Press Synopsis: Section One has Nikita arrested and sent to prison in order to discover the identity of a human time bomb.

Episode #33: "Psychic Pilgrim"

Written by Michael Loceff
Directed by Rene Bonnierre
Guest Starring Joaquimde Almeida, Susan
    Kottmann, Marcus Spilotro, and Christopher
    Clements

Press Synopsis: Nikita poses as a psychic in order to discover information on an upcoming terrorist attack. Meanwhile, Madeline is preoccupied with thoughts of her dying mother.

CONFIDENTIAL

IDIOT'S GUIDE
TO SECTION ONE

USA Network/Shooting Star

CONTENTS

FOREWORD

This guide has been designed specifically for new recruits into what is commonly referred to as Section One. This organization is a covert group of convicted felons, including murderers, thieves, sociopaths, and various other misfits, all with access now to the latest in military hardware, software, and generally anything high-tech and covert. Frightening, isn't it? Anyway, to fit quickly into the Section's organizational framework, it is recommended that this book be read cover to cover, as Madeline will be quizzing you on various sections throughout your training.

Note: Any full-fledged operative caught reading this book will be deemed an idiot and therefore a potential "problem" and can be the subject of a "cancellation" request.

Terri Malinski (codename: Tel)
Section Two Operative

CHAPTER 1

Section Terminology

Before beginning our little foray into Section One, a discussion of the various acronyms and terminology used at the Section will be most helpful to the new recruit.

1) Agency: Home of the big muckety-mucks that even Ops (Operations) occasionally reports to

2) Close-quarter standby: When all available operatives stand as close as possible while watching terrorist TV

3) Cold mission: One in which you will be cold and probably need a coat

4) Com set: A set of comic books Birkoff keeps under his bed for serious reading

5) Dead con scenario: Any time a convict gets dead and Section personnel have to figure out how he got perished

6) Floating backup teams: Operatives who float on their backs in the pool (otherwise known as wet operatives)

7) Go live: Opposite of stop dead

8) Innocent: Usually a pizza deliveryman unaware that Section is not a location on the delivery route

9) Intel: Computer-chip manufacturer in California that Birkoff has stock in (actually we think he owns it, but he's not tellin')

10) Material: What Section clothing is made of

11) Planted: What we do with trees

12) Warm mission: Just the opposite of a cold mission, probably in the tropics. A swimsuit is recommended.

13) Downtime: Time not spent on a mission. This is when you have nothing to do and usually get really bored.

Please review these terms and become familiar with them. They will be used throughout your training and eventual life at Section One. Next we will take you on a little tour of the Section. . . .

CHAPTER 2

Getting Around the Section

For the new recruit, finding your way around Section One can be daunting at times. Therefore, a walking tour of the Section will be provided below for your benefit. Please remember to wear comfortable shoes, and don't forget your bag of breadcrumbs so if you get lost, you can find your way back (providing you've been dropping said breadcrumbs along the route).

We start our walking tour at the BIG DOORS. Yes, these are BIG DOORS! FIREPROOF BIG DOORS! BOMBPROOF BIG DOORS! And just generally BIG DOORS, no matter how you slice it. If you look at the dimly lit corridor in front of you, you will notice two small passageways on either side of this main entrance (i.e.: THE BIG DOORS). These are service entrances for the bottled-water guy, the Coke guy, and the Pepsi dude to use to restock the machines in the cafeteria. (Oh, did we forget to tell you we have a cafeteria? You didn't hear it from me!) Why do we have two passageways you ask? The Pepsi dude doesn't like the Coke guy, and so we have two passageways so they each can take one. The bottled-water guy's liked by both, so he can use whichever passageway is closest to his water mobile.

Walking straight ahead (watch out for the low water pipes—they don't really have water in them but they add to the dark basement look, don't you think?) we come to the first corridor that anyone really uses. To the left of the main corridor (the BIG DOORS are behind us) is the garage. This is where we park our van. (The Pepsi dude always tries to sneak in this way 'cause it's closer to the cafeteria, but we don't let him!) There are lots of cool-looking light-boards above the garage door (well, actually it's more like a vault door 'cause we couldn't get the Genie garage door to work properly, so Birkoff gave up). The words and letters that flash across really don't mean anything but they sure look cool! Unfortunately, we can't go into the garage today since Birkoff is having a six-disc CD changer installed.

Walking past the garage (BIG DOORS are still behind us), to the right is the cafeteria. The cafeteria is very high-tech looking. Stainless steel counters, concrete floors and ceilings, very modern chairs and tables. Too bad the food tastes like slop! And the cook can't make a decent cup of coffee to save his life. That's why we have the Coke and Pepsi machines! Michael's always complaining about the coffee. We've tried to get him to drink Pepsi, but he just keeps whining about the coffee anyway. Course he won't volunteer to make any himself, just whine, whine, whine. Oh sorry, I digress.

You will notice two small doors next to the cafeteria. These are the only rest rooms on this side of the Section. Unfortunately, when there are quite a few operatives returning from a mission and the food has been exceptionally horrible in the cafeteria that day, these can be quite crowded. Lines have been known to form outside and wrap around the cafeteria. My suggestion: Try to make it to the other end of the Section, if you can.

The main corridor takes a turn to the left, just after the bathrooms, and opens into a large lobby area. Notice the subdued color theme here. Black! The security guard's name is Fred, and he's really nice, provided you know where you want to go and have the proper clearance to go there (no I don't mean the bathrooms, either!). Behind Fred you'll see three corridors to choose from. Corridor one, to the left of Fred, contains R&D and the hospital.

The R&D area is where Section thinks up all those nifty little gadgets you'll eventually get to play with when you become an operative. Things like exploding lipstick, exploding gum, exploding toilet paper tubes (well, that one didn't go over too well—Ops got a beta version by accident) and other interesting things we'll cover in chapter 5, Things That Go Bang, and chapter 6, Things That Go Beep. Suffice it to say that this is a really cool place to sneak a peek into, if you can.

Opposite the R&D area (and good thing, too) is the hospital wing. We have all sorts of shiny instruments in here, pretty sliding glass doors, and many monitors that beep and display squiggly readouts that no one really understands. But they look important, so we keep them around for looks. When you get shot (see chapter 9, What to Do When You've Been Shot), you'll be brought here, and many people in white lab coats will insert cold steel into orifices you didn't know you had. Don't say I didn't warn you! This place always has a funny smell, so avoid it if you can.

The middle corridor behind Fred is the office area. Walking this way, we first come to Birkoff's room. We're not allowed in there, and actually, you don't *want* to go in there, either. Gets pretty weird in there around Halloween. Actually, it got pretty weird in there when *MST,* the movie, came out, too, so we try to leave him alone. Sometimes he comes out with underwear on his head and we just don't ask anymore. Be prepared!

Moving on very quickly, the next office is Michael's. His office is rather small and spartan, but very functional! He tried to have us paint the walls and ceiling black like the floor, but we thought that was overkill, even for him. So he got gray instead, as a compromise. His office overlooks the operative training area, with which you are very familiar by now. Across from the training area is the laser-tag arena. We've told you this is to test your reflexes in the field, but actually, we *do* use it just for laser tag. When you become a full operative, you can join one of our four laser-tag teams. We hold monthly tournaments with the Agency and Cleaners teams, and so far have whopped their butts. The Cleaners are really bad sports, so just watch yourself. They have a penchant for tossing acid around after a particularly humiliating loss, so if they offer to shake your hand after you've killed them for the twelfth time, I'd decline if I were you. Ops takes personal pride in the fact that we've won the last five interagency tournaments, so if you want to earn brownie points with the big kahuna, better practice up.

Walking past the laser-tag area, you will see a large unmarked door. This is the interrogation room. It looks like a vault, and essentially it is. Soundproof, all white, sterile, only a chair in the center of the room. Kinda like the principal's office at school in your worst nightmare. It is a very bad thing to be an interrogatee in this room. Most people who go in don't come out with all their original appendages attached. Operatives have been known to be "canceled" in this room, so if someone invites you in there for a "friendly game of strip poker" . . . be suspicious!

At the very end of the corridor, we come to the double doors of Madeline's office. This office looks like a medieval dungeon with good reason—it is! (Well, OK, it's actually the remnants of an old subway tunnel, but we like to pretend it is.) Madeline likes the depressing look—it helps her psyche out the operatives. Plus, she had lots of antiques anyway, so they fit in well with the general decor. The cool thing about Madeline's doors are that they open up automatically, even though they have door knockers. Since we couldn't get the garage door opener to work properly, Walter modified it for use on her door. Cool, huh?

This completes this corridor. Walking back to Fred (who's not used to seeing a confused group of recruits walking single file and holding hands so no one gets lost), we approach the final corridor. This will take us to the heart of Section One.

Walking through the narrow corridor, it opens up into the cavernous expanse of the nerve center of Section One, the computer room, the briefing-staging area, the weapons arsenal, and last but not least Operations' Control Room. And oh yeah, THE OTHER SET OF BATHROOMS!

The first area we see as we walk into this center is the long table used for briefings. This is the briefing area and the wide-open space behind it is the staging area. When Ops isn't around, we have roller hockey games here. If you decide to play, just be careful, the floor is slick and once Chuck (poor dead Chuck—we miss him dearly) slid right into one of the glass doors to the computer room, shattering it. We spent all night picking up glass and cleaning the scratches off the floor so Ops wouldn't know what we'd been up to. Make sure your brakes are in working order.

The computer room is next up. This is Birkoff's home away from home, and he's very picky about his computers. No one touches anything here without his authorization (especially any paused video games or the bowl of Oreos—to touch either one is certain death). We're not really sure what all these computers and monitors do but they look neat, especially when we can get them to all flash red at the same time! You will also notice the rows of CD-ROMs sitting on top of the desks. Birkoff is a big fan of 80s rock (as is Ops), so we have a complete collection of the works of Duran Duran, Frankie Goes to Hollywood, and INXS, just to name a few. You will often notice Birkoff and one of the other comtechs intently studying the monitors on the far side of the computer room. No, they're not running some top secret defcon scenario—they're actually playing Quake. Birkoff hacked into ID software and stole their beta version of the new online multi-player upgrade for Quake and had it hidden from Ops in a special directory on the mainframe listed as Office Supplies. If you open up the Three-Ring Binder file under Office Supplies, it gets you into the game. Birkoff's the top frag player this month, taking the title from Michael who'd been the top fragger for several month's running.

If you look up from the computer area, you'll notice a long glass room above you. This is the control room, better know as Ops' Place. Ops monitors all the goings-on at Section One from here (yes even the bathrooms!). All the computers are hooked up to monitors in this room so Ops can pace back and forth and worry for the rest of us. The view is actually quite nice from up there, so if you ever get the opportunity to sneak in and take a look, I recommend it. Just try not to have to go up there on official business—that usually means you're gonna get yelled at or worse!

Walking to the right of the computer area, we have the weapons room (better known internally as Walter's Toy Shop). In here you'll find guns, ammunition, gas masks, bazookas, slingshots, crossbows, blowguns, and just about anything else dangerous to mankind. Walter's pretty picky about his stuff, though, so be careful what you take, and make sure you put it back (except for the ammunition and used blow darts). Walter does have a checkout system for this stuff, but we've never figured out what it really is, and he seems to forget most of the time, too. Usually asking nicely will be enough to get you what you want.

Lastly, on the left side of the computer area is the OTHER SET OF BATHROOMS. The lines here aren't usually as long as those by the cafeteria, so if you can hold it, these bathrooms are the better bet. Plus, they're cleaner, too. Computer personnel seem to be more conscientious about this than other Section personnel.

This completes our tour of Section One. Familiarize yourself with the layout. Ops takes a dim view of recruits who get lost. Speaking of Ops, in chapter 3 we will talk about people to avoid.

CHAPTER 3

People to Avoid

As you, the new recruit, become more familiar with the inner workings of the Section, you will realize that everyone has days when they're best left alone. Nikita, when she's having a bad-hair day, is a typical example. However, there are certain people at the Section that are best avoided, if possible. For these particular individuals, contact is best made only when requested, and then be brief, answer succinctly the questions posed to you directly, and above all, don't joke around—these people have absolutely no sense of humor.

OPERATIONS: Operations, or Ops as he's nicknamed in the Section, is one individual everyone agrees should be avoided at all costs. He doesn't like the majority of operatives and finds them a necessary evil in the pursuit of the Section's prime directives. However, to him, operatives have the same importance as Kleenex—to be used, then discarded when they can't perform their job satisfactorily anymore. He also has no sense of humor and takes a dim view of some of the antics that go on at the Section during "close quarters" when all operatives are on-site. Bottom line: Don't put this guy on your e-mail joke list!

However, it must be emphasized that from time to time, you will be brought into the control room for a little "discussion" with Ops concerning training, mission status, agent cancellation, and the like. Be prepared to answer his questions completely, clearly (he hates mumblers), and to the point. The sooner he can get you out of his sight, the better.

MICHAEL: Many are surprised that we include Michael on our list of people to be avoided. While under most circumstances Michael doesn't need to be avoided, there are a few instances you need to be aware of. If he's in one of these states, turn the other direction and walk quickly to the nearest exit (or hide in the bathroom, whichever is closest):

1) When he hasn't had his coffee yet this morning. Let's face it, Michael is a grouch without his first cup of coffee. He's been

known to slam doors, smack the back of people's heads (just ask Birkoff), and generally order operatives into senseless, suicidal missions (just ask Chuck) when he's caffeineless. We usually try to have a cup of Irish Creme waiting for him at his desk in the morning just to avoid any unpleasantries. When it's your turn to make it, don't complain. It's easier on everyone!

2) When he has the cafeteria coffee instead of his Irish Creme. I know what you're thinking—caffeine is caffeine, coffee is coffee, so what's the big deal? We don't know either! All we know is, when he has the cafeteria coffee he whines about how bad it is, how he doesn't like it, how Irish Creme is better, and on and on and on. Yet he never volunteers to make *us* a pot of Irish Creme! Oh no, that would be too civil! No, just spouts and complains and usually stomps off to slam another door. Course, what do we expect? This is the same guy that whines about the coffee, yet takes the last cup and won't make a fresh pot for anyone else to drink! So when he's like this—just let him whine. Eventually, someone will make him a cup of Irish Creme (usually Nikita, 'cause she can't stand it anymore than the rest of us), and he's OK after that.

COKE GUY or **PEPSI DUDE:** Depends on which you like more. These two hate each other and relish trying to sabotage the other's machine. If you get caught in the middle of one of their soda wars it's worse than being interrogated by Ops. What we usually do is note what day the deliveries are gonna be made and then find some terrorist to track down and perish while they're loading up the machines in the cafeteria. This seems to work well and we avoid any of their unpleasantries. One word of advice: If you do happen to get cornered by one of them and they begin to interrogate you as to which you prefer best, Coke or Pepsi, the safest reply is that you're a bottled-water person and really don't drink soda. The bottled-water guy is pretty much neutral (sorta like Switzerland), so he's a safe bet.

INTERNAL SECURITY OPERATIVES (better known as **CLEANERS**): Let's face it, these people are just plain bad news. They're the best of the best that the Agency and the Section have to offer, and they have no sense of humor whatsoever. I don't think they even know how to spell the word! You usually don't see them around much (which is good), but lately with all this hoopla about the directory, they've been seen around more and more. Usually they work outside the Section and only get involved in Section operations when there's been a breach of internal security or a mission has been botched. You can recognize a Cleaner by the all-black fatigues worn any time of the year. They're usually armed to the teeth and take great delight in harassing Operations (which actually isn't such a bad thing!). Pray they never have to interrogate you for anything, but if they do, follow the same procedure as with Ops—be direct, succinct, and don't joke. One other thing to add is don't look at them directly, either. They're very good at staring you down, which will undoubtedly make you more nervous, resulting in your likely telling them what they want to hear whether it's the truth or not. We usually try to look really busy whenever they're around, even if it means doing all that paperwork we've been putting off for the last six months.

As you can see, there aren't very many people to avoid in the Section, but they can really mess your day up if you run into them unprepared. Keep this in mind next time you round a corridor and see one of them.

On a brighter side, there are many people at the Section that can help you immensely to become a better operative and simply keep you alive. In chapter 4 we'll discuss people to be nice to.

CHAPTER 4

People to Be Nice To

In the Section there are many factions, each competing for supremacy. For the new recruit, learning which side is politically correct that week can spell the difference between a long life and a short trip to an interrogation room (or worse!). To ensure your continued good health, learning who to be nice to (now that you know who to avoid) becomes the number one goal of your training. These people can help you in your career at Section or can send you on a one-way mission to oblivion. Being nice to everyone is good manners—being nice to the right person is critical to survival.

With that in mind, of all the people in the Section, there are only a few you need to take special care of and be really nice to.

FRED: Yep. Heard me right—Fred the security guard. Why be nice to him, you ask? Because he's the eyes and ears of Ops in this part of Section. Plus, he controls the property passes. You wanna take that laptop home to play one of Birkoff's multiuser Doom or Quake games—you gotta get through Fred. Fred gets chocolates on Valentine's Day, a present at Christmas, candy at Easter and Halloween, and a card on his birthday (June 2). If you're not nice to Fred—Ops will know, and he won't be happy either (see last chapter). So better be safe than sorry—suck up to Fred.

WALTER: We at Section consider Walter sorta like Santa Claus. But instead of bringing us Barbie dolls and Nintendo, he brings us bazookas and AK-16 assault rifles with full cartridges, bombs, and Kevlar vests. Much better than Santa, we think! Walter's pretty easy-going most of the time, but if you get on his bad side, you may just wind up with the Kevlar vest with a hole in the back, courtesy of Michael, or get the Uzi that jams every time you fire. It's actually pretty easy to be nice to Walter. For the female operative, a short skirt or a lace teddy just showing underneath a shirt is usually enough. For the male operative, bringing him a new roll of duct tape, copper and gold wire, or a new box of detonators should be enough to endear you to him through at least the next mission. However, the male operative needs to realize that Walter's favoritism will dwindle along with the detonators, so be prepared with plenty of things to constantly restock his supply cabinet.

(Last but not least)

BIRKOFF: Though Birkoff may not seem like anyone you need to take special care to be nice to, as a new recruit you need to understand Birkoff's importance in the Section. Birkoff runs the missions from his computer or laptop (if he's on the road with us). As the mission specialist, he's responsible for monitoring your position out in the field and ensuring you're adequately protected by jamming radio frequencies and also monitoring enemy movements. While this job is vital to the success of the operatives in the field, Birkoff has a much more important function within the Section. You see, Birkoff is also responsible for maintaining your credit card and checking account balances. Get on his bad side, and you're likely to have your checks bounce or have your VISA card rejected at the mall. While this can be a pain at home, it's really irritating when you're in Costa Rica trying to buy mosquito repellent or in Sydney trying to buy Nikita a new pair of sunglasses. But even more critical than controlling your credit card and checking account, Birkoff also controls your access to the games directory on the Section's computer system. Mess with this guy and you'll be locked out of Doom, won't be able to participate in the multiplayer Quake tournaments we run each month, and you can kiss your high score in Duke Nukem goodbye.

The good news is that Birkoff is the easiest (and cheapest) person to be nice to. A new bag of Oreos will usually do the trick. If you really want to suck up to him for extra points, spring for a new joystick (the multimovement ones used for Flight Simulator), or buy him the 1000-level expansion module to Duke Nukem (he's been wanting that one for a while).

So as you can see, there aren't many people in Section that you have to make a special effort to be nice to. Most people in the Section can be happily ignored with no adverse effects to your well-being. But for those we have listed, it is advised to begin sucking up ASAP because the sooner you do, the more points you earn (kinda like frequent-flyer miles). The more points, the better the stuff you get, and this can make the difference between being a live operative or a dead one. If I were you, I'd pick live over dead any day! Don't be embarrassed about sucking up either—we all do it, and given the alternative are quite happy to do so. Besides, that 1000-level expansion pack is pretty hot!

This concludes our discussion of the people skills required to become a successful Section One operative. Now we'll turn our attention to the tools of the trade in chapter 5, with a discussion of things that go bang.

CHAPTER 5

Things That Go Bang

There are many skills required to become a successful operative here at Section One. One of the most important aspects of the job, of course (and the one most of us like the best), is killing things. The most common weapon we use to perish things is the gun, or as we call it: that thing that goes bang.

There are many types of things that go bang (e.g., guns). We actually have different guns for different occasions and missions.

The most common gun the majority of Section operatives use is a standard military-issue 9mm handgun with optional silencer attachment. As a new recruit, you will be issued this type of weapon (live ammunition comes later). The reason this is the weapon of choice for most operatives is that any fool can use it. It's easy to handle, light enough to aim fairly accurately, and it doesn't take a brain surgeon to figure out how to shoot with it. Walter is particularly fond of it because he unfortunately often gets stuck with manning the firing range for new recruits (like you). A quick five-minute lecture on this baby and you're off blasting holes in faraway pieces of paper. Plus, it looks way cooler to whip out than most of the other guns we stock (except for the bazooka—but more on that later).

Another, more sophisticated, weapon used by only a few operatives is the Walther PPK. We never used to stock this gun, but Michael—in one of his weird moods—wanted to feel like James

Bond, so he specifically asked for it. We all laughed at that, but hey, he's the boss, so he gets what he wants. He even did the "Bond, James Bond" routine too! Really funny! (Actually, he used to have a really good sense of humor, until Simone died. We keep hoping someday he'll get it back again 'cause he really can be a funny guy!) So bottom line with this weapon is we've got it but you can't have it.

We do have a couple of .357 Magnums in stock, too, but they're just way too loud and bulky to use on a regular basis. Just try stuffin' that little beauty into an evening bag, I dare you! Walter loves this one though. Sometime, late at night after everyone's gone if you're still around (and Fred hasn't kicked you out yet), see if you can get him to do his Dirty Harry imitation. It's really quite good!

If you like more rapid-fire hardware, then the Uzi may be more to your liking. The internal security operatives are usually the ones getting first dibs on these guys. A bit more bulky than the handgun, but hey, if you're not gonna conceal it and want to go purely for looks, then this is the gun for you. An Uzi makes a great first impression on anyone you intend to fill full of holes.

Walter does stock several styles of rifles, and if you are chosen as a stationary point during a mission, then you will probably be issued one of these. They tend to be cumbersome to use without extensive practice, but the laser sight makes up for this. Just remember that these guys recoil, so don't do the Rambo thing and hold it too close to an appendage you don't want bruised.

Finally, my favorite of all things that go bang is the bazooka (the gun, not the bubblegum). While technically this weapon is classed under things that go boom, I include it here simply because it fires essentially like a rifle. The only thing to remember here is which side fires the projectile. Yes, we did have a new recruit who eighty-sixed the target shed when he fired the wrong end! After that incident, Walter stenciled instructions on each one, with arrows that say "This end outward (to bad guy)" and the other end that says "This end toward you (good guy)." The instructions just say point and click (inside joke here). We're trying to make Walter PC-literate; so when he was stenciling the instructions, he thought he'd show us how much he'd learned.

Well, that essentially completes our section on things that go bang. We do have several other weapons that go thunk (crossbow), thwap (blowgun), and thud (knives); but with the exception of the knives, these are rarely used. Next up, we'll discuss things that go boom, in chapter 6.

CHAPTER 6
Things That Go Beep

I know you're wondering why in the last chapter we said chapter 6 would be "Things That Go Boom" and now we're saying it's "Things That Go Beep." Well, two reasons: 1) We've used up all the things that go boom, thanks to Michael, who used our last bazooka shell on those doors to Lisa's house instead of just kicking them in! 2) We liked the things with the beepy noises better. Besides, as a new recruit you can be canceled for asking questions like this. So onward!

As an operative, you will occasionally be given additional equipment to successfully complete your mission. In this chapter, we will describe several of our more interesting things that go beep and discuss their uses in a mission. Study this chapter carefully and become familiar with their operation.

Beeping Makeup Sample Case: This is Madeline's least favorite piece of equipment. This makeup sample case has a large transmitter in the false bottom that beeps loudly to inform you and any bad guys you're talking to that you have an incoming transmission. The transmitter is easy to access and operate. Just pull out the eyeshadow and blush, and there it is. Luckily too, it beeps loudly and continuously to give you plenty of time to dig through the makeup to get to the transmitter and shut it off. Chuck used to use it (when he was still alive) as an alarm clock.

Beeping Sneaker Ball-Bomb: While this is technically a thing that goes boom, it beeps before it booms, so we put it here, too. This little cutie packs a wallop and emits a cutsie beepy noise for thirty seconds before it booms. This is usually used in the enemy's closet to distract and confuse him. Just pop one or two into a pair of tennis shoes and you're set. Plus they deodorize before they explode! They're also great to liven up dull parties.

Beeping Nikita Tracker: Michael's personal favorite! This tracker picks up a signal from Nikita's boots and let's you know where she is at all times. We finally had to have Walter rig this up for her because she's always getting into trouble of some sort. One nice additional feature is that it plays all Game Boy software, too!

Beeping Lipstick-Holder Remote Detonator: While the lipstick itself is made of plastique, the holder is the remote detonator. Comes in handy when you're on a date and the guy is being really rude. Just leave the tube at the table, take the holder to the ladies room and *KABOOM!* No more date! The detonator tube emits a cheery beep, and the ultramodel will also do a verbal countdown from ten, with the additional comment at one of "one second till lipstick limbo." Michael and the guys don't get it, but Nikita and the rest of us gals get a hoot out of it!

Beeping Team Finder: Ever been on a mission and accidentally misplace your team? Well, this will never happen again with the Beeping Team Finder. Just attach the accompanying blue dots to all team members, and when the finder is activated, they magically appear on the screen showing you just how far off you screwed up! For new recruits like you, this is very helpful during parachute drops when you weren't paying attention when everyone else jumped and you wind up miles from the action. Just don't let Ops know you're using it too often or you could be canceled for incompetence.

Beeping Computer Screen Saver: This was one of Birkoff's best inventions yet! Since we all enjoy the team Doom and Quake competitions, much to Ops's irritation, this screen saver will automatically signal that command personnel are in the area and immediately replace your Doom or Quake game on the screen with an EXCEL spreadsheet or sim output (whichever you prefer). This is great when you're in a heated game and just can't quit. So far Ops hasn't caught on to this tactic, and we hope he doesn't for some time, because we're currently going for the team high score in Quake, and Birkoff's gonna be really upset if we get caught and have to start from scratch. So use this one with caution, but it is available for general operative use!

That completes our tour of the things that go beep in Section One. This also completes our overall tour of Section One. In the remaining chapters we will be discussing preparation for your first mission, what to look out for, and fun things to do. To begin with, we'll be discussing why we operatives hate red, in chapter 7: Why Red Is a Bad Color.

CHAPTER 7

Why Red Is a Bad Color

For many of us here at Section One, *Star Trek* is our favorite TV series. Sometimes during close quarters, we all gather at Birkoff's place and watch our favorite episodes on tape. Have you ever noticed that the away team members with the red shirts always seem to die? We have! Correlation you ask? Well, Section One also has it's own version of these same away team members.

We call these operatives Red Shirt Operatives, or RSOs for short. These operatives are generally recruit washouts or simply operatives considered expendable for some reason by Operations and Madeline. If you looked in their files (which of course you can't because you're a new recruit and not authorized, but *if* you could), you would see that all of them have a psychological defect that eliminates them from being prime operative material. Remember that recruit that Nikita was evaluating, Karyn what's-her-name? Proves my point!

So why have RSOs you wonder? Sometimes we need someone for the bad guys to aim at so the real operatives can get through and complete the mission. RSOs come in handy for this. Just put them out in front, at point, and watch the bad guys plug away. If you're lucky, the RSO may actually get a few shots off and take out a bad guy or two for you. But mostly they're just considered cannon fodder (or Bantha fodder if you're into *Star Wars* like Birkoff!)

Older operatives can turn into RSOs as well as new recruits. Screw up one too many times and there'll be a red shirt waiting for you on your next mission. Sometimes a new recruit unknowingly selects a red garment for an undercover mission. Madeline will usually smirk but not say a word about it and just wait to see if the operative returns in one piece. If you happen to make this often fatal mistake, the only advice I can give you is to watch your back as well as your front. Since we figure the RSOs are gonna die anyway, we're not too careful where we aim. So, *watch out!!* If you survive, the mistake is usually never made again. Why do you think Michael almost always wears black? Lesson learned; what can I say?

So remember, next time Madeline tells you to pick out a garment to wear, leave the red alone. She will be very impressed that you're not as naive as you look. Also, if you happen to have an RSO on a mission with you, just remember they make excellent body shields. So stick to black—it's great camouflage at night, looks good on everyone, and hides dirt really well.

Now that you're color savvy, we will continue with your new recruit preparation in chapter 8, Preparing for Your First Mission.

CHAPTER 8

Preparing for Your First Mission

If you've made it this far into training, you're well on your way to becoming a first-class operative. Congratulations! In this chapter we'll take you step-by-step into everything you need to know to prepare adequately for, and survive, your first mission.

First you need to select the appropriate clothes to wear (remember the advice in chapter 7 and avoid red at all costs!). For your first mission, you may be lucky and Madeline might select clothing for you. If not, we recommend a color selection of black (or at worst, camouflage) so you can hide really well against white backgrounds. For night missions, we recommend ski clothing with the corresponding black ski masks. You can't see a darn thing in them, but they look very spyish, so that's why we use them.

Next, a trip to Walter's Toy Shop is in order. Again, Walter may be nice enough to select an assortment of weapons for you. If not, the type of mission will determine what you need to take along. A 9mm handgun is always a good bet because any idiot can use it. If you think you'll need to bust down some doors, ask Walter for the bazooka (why scuff perfectly good boots?). If you're feeling really adventuresome, you might pack along a couple of hand grenades and a throwing knife or two. We don't use them much but they sure do look cool hanging from your belt.

Next stop is Birkoff for the mission profile if you weren't at the briefing (which almost no one ever attends except Michael, Nikita, and a couple of RSOs). He'll supply you with maps, suggested position points and extraction locations. If you're lucky, he'll supply you with some of his gadgets that look really high tech but are totally useless. (He's the computer whiz, not the gadget guru like Walter, but we just can't bring ourselves to tell him that. So we smile, take them, and throw them in the back of the van.)

Now you're almost ready to board the van. One stop left. The bathroom. Michael gets really irritated when we have to stop at a gas station or on the side of the road because someone forgot to go. And believe me, he'll ask everyone before we leave, so start off on his good side and just go before you board!

As you get in the van, look up and notice the light-board above your head. The board has totally useless information on it because no one can figure out how to code it. Yes, we can defuse nuclear weapons and take down terrorists, but we can't program our own light-board. We keep hoping Birkoff will crack the code someday, but for now we just let it flash anything it wants to. Sometimes it actually does make coherent sentences. It does this just to confuse us and make us think we'll actually get useful information out of it some-day. But for now, ignore the gibberish on it and get in the van.

Once in the van, there's a couple of rules you need to know and abide by. First off, there's a seat assignment order. Michael sits by the door (when he's in back with us). Birkoff, when he goes, sits across from Michael. Walter sits next to Birkoff, and Nikita sits next to Michael (of course!). New recruits sit at the back of the van. There are only two seats with seat belts, so you might want to grab one of them. Sometimes the ride gets pretty bumpy, and we have had RSOs hit the side of the van and die. So rule number one is: Head to the back of the van and buckle up!

Van rule number two: No eating or drinking in the van. Walter takes great care of the van and gets really sore at anyone caught leav-ing crumbs and stains on the carpet. Plus, the crumbs can get into the keyboard and ruin Birkoff's latest game of Quake, which he usu-ally plays on the way to the drop-off point. So eat before you go.

Van rule number three: Don't ask questions about the van's dri-ver. There isn't one! We don't exactly know how the van gets to the drop-off point, we think it has something to do with the light-board back at Section. We're still not sure what the correlation is, but all we know is we get where we need to be. Just so we don't freak out drivers and passersby with a driverless van, Michael sometimes sits in the front, so when people ask questions or tell us we can't park here, he can smack their heads into the door. He really enjoys that!

Once you're dropped off, there's no talking unless Michael, Nikita, or Birkoff requests information. No telling jokes, no making cutsie remarks about girls or guys walking by, and above all, no asking for a potty break (you were supposed to go before you left!).

The only other thing to remember on your first mission is to stay alive! Dying is so permanent! It can really put a dent into your day and ruin any chances of promotion. The best way to ensure you stay in one piece is to keep an RSO (you know, the operatives wearing the red shirts) in front of you at all times. Remember, they make great body shields (see chapter 7).

So be careful. Listen to Michael, Nikita, Birkoff, and Walter, and follow their instructions. Keep your head down. Keep an RSO in front of you at all times. Make sure the safety catch is off your gun and have fun!

Even the best-prepared missions can go awry on occasion. In chapter 9 we'll cover an inevitability of life in the Section, or what to do when you've been shot.

CHAPTER 9

What to Do When You've Been Shot

OK. So you did all the things we told you to do in chapter 8, you thought you were doing just fine, and *bingo!* Some SOTW (Slime of the Week) gets lucky and shoots you! Now what?

IDIOT'S GUIDE TO SECTION ONE

First of all, DON'T PANIC! Let your training take over. Sure this hurts way worse than laser tag. Sure you're leaking vital body fluid all over the street, tarmac, or wherever you happen to be. Sure that stain isn't going to come out with just soap and water. But then again, no one said this job was gonna be easy! So take a deep breath (if you can, unless you've been shot in the chest) and know that help will be here soon.

Next, you need to notify Michael, Nikita, or Birkoff that you've been shot. Don't go screaming into the van yelling, "I've been shot! I've been shot!" You'll needlessly panic the RSOs, agitate everyone else in the van, and wear yourself out. Simply use your com set and let someone know that the RSO you were using as a body shield didn't work and you need extraction fast! Someone competent will be there soon (hopefully). While you're waiting, it is a good idea to grab the nearest RSO and use them to soak up any stray bullets that might be flying your way. No need to get any extra holes in you if you can help it.

When you get to the van, try not to bleed on the floor or the seats. Remember what I said in the last chapter? Walter really gets ticked when there's bloodstains on the carpet, because they don't come out easily! We usually keep paper towels and a spare rag or two under one of the chairs, so grab some and stuff them into the holes to stop the bleeding. Or, if you prefer, and the bullet went all the way through the wound, Michael can cauterize the wound to stop the bleeding. Based on past personal experience, he's a real expert in this area.

Once you're safely back at the Section, you'll be put on a stretcher if the wound is severe (otherwise you'll walk), and be taken to the

Section hospital. Here, people in white lab coats will hover around you, prodding instruments into orifices in your body, and poke at the bullet wound with shiny metal objects. Then they'll hook you up to machines that make those bleepy noises. We're told these people all have medical degrees of some sort, but we're not really sure if that's true. They forever seem intent on doing whatever it takes to get the machine to stop making that stupid bleepy noise. But they are nice, and I'm sure you'll feel better after your visit.

Next stop is the recovery room. This room is all white with all sorts of interesting monitors and machines to check out. The bad thing about this room is that the beds are generally about six inches too short, so you wind up having to scrunch up your legs just to fit. When Michael's been in here, we usually can't get him to lie down long enough to worry about how short the bed is. But when Nikita's been in here, she generally finds it easier to hang her feet over the edge, lie with her knees sticking up, or curl up into a fetal position to sleep. One of those positions should work for you, too. Unfortunately, there's no TV in here, so be prepared to sleep a lot or read a good book because you're gonna get bored. But I'm sure you'll have visitors. Nikita's great at visiting operatives who have been wounded on a mission with her; and Michael will come by to get a status report from you for Ops. Who knows, if I can, I'll stop by, too, and check up on you.

Hopefully, you'll never have to experience what we've just discussed in this chapter. But as you know, sometimes things go wrong. Then again, sometimes they go *very wrong*. Next we'll discuss what happens when things do go very wrong, in chapter 10, What Housekeeping Really Means (or Why We Hate Cleaners).

CHAPTER 10

What Housekeeping Really Means (or Why We Hate Cleaners)

As we said in the last chapter, no matter how carefully you plan a mission, it's an inevitable fact of life that on occasion things will go wrong. Most of the time when things go wrong, we operatives are resourceful enough to fix it. However, sometimes the mess is so big that we can't. When that kind of situation happens, the very existence of the Section can be compromised. This is serious business and calls for a serious solution! So who ya gonna call? No, not Ghostbusters, housekeeping!

Housekeeping? What's housekeeping got to do with Section One, you ask? I know it sounds a lot like being in a hotel. But, unlike the housekeeping staff at your local Hyatt, these guys don't wipe down your toilet (unless there's some dead guy in it), they don't make your bed, and they don't give you service with a smile. Our housekeeping staff (nicknamed "Cleaners") are called in when we've screwed up so badly that we can't fix it ourselves. If they have to be called in to finish the job, or cleanup, you're in BIG trouble!

So, you ask, who are Cleaners and why haven't you seen any around Section? Well, Cleaners are a group of operatives separate from the rest of us. They are handpicked and the best of us in terms of accuracy, speed, and above all, ruthlessness. They are no-nonsense operatives, totally without emotion, and have absolutely no sense of humor, either (gee, kinda sounds like Michael, huh?). You've probably seen them around Section, returning from a cleanup, but didn't realize it. They're easy to spot. They look like a standard team with black military fatigues (unless they're undercover), but their fatigues have a tiny skull-and-crossbones patch on their left sleeve. Very dramatic, but also very functional. They don't want to be confused with any of us, and we don't want to make that mistake either!

These operatives (and yes, there are female Cleaners, too; and no, they don't wear maid's uniforms so don't even try that joke with them!) are bad news. Borderline psychotics, actually. Looking at them, they don't look very threatening, which is often why they're so good at what they do. They don't look like they could hurt a fly. However, looks can be deceiving. These people have been known to pour acid on faces, cut off fingers, shoot people in the back of the head (all before breakfast!). We're all slightly afraid of these people— even Ops, but he'll never let you know it! However, they know it, too, and use it to their advantage around here.

One of their favorite pastimes at Section, when they're around, is picking fights with us substandard operatives (at least, that's what they call us). A typical ploy is to walk into the cafeteria and begin complaining about the food, the service, the guns, the training, and then the operatives themselves. We tend to think of them as the neighborhood bullies, and as with all bullies, we just ignore them and go about our business. Generally, when they realize you won't take the bait, they get disgusted and leave you alone and go off in search of some other prey. The only one of us who ever took the bait and whopped one of these guys real good was, you guessed it, Michael. Yeah, one of these guys had the stupidity to pick a fight with Michael by calling him "incompetent." (Must have got that little gem from Petrosian!) Anyway, Michael went off the deep end and knocked the guy's teeth out! In all fairness, it had been a particularly bad day for him: We ran out of Irish Creme coffee, he got yelled at by Ops for something, and with just ten thousand points to go to break the high score on Duke Nukem his laptop crashed! But even he doesn't recommend confronting these guys, bad day or not!

Okay, so these guys are bad news. Avoid them if possible, ignore them when taunted. So why do we need them around anyway? What exactly do they do to "clean up?" Well, if you missed a hit or left bodies where you shouldn't have, the Cleaners will be called in to finish the job and clean up the mess. They will quickly finish the hit, and/or terminate anyone that might have seen you, wipe off fingerprints, take any articles you've accidentally left behind (for return to Madeline or Walter), and wipe up any bloodstains. When they're done, you won't be able to tell anything unusual went on. In terms of efficiency and speed, bullies or not, they're very good at what they do.

One other function they perform (kinda for grins) is cancellations. Ops felt it was better if the standard operatives didn't perform cancellations for moral reasons. I mean, how could you trust someone that just offed your best operative bud? So it was felt a "neutral" party should do it. There is usually one Cleaner stationed on standby in Section just for this reason. They rotate every month so you never know which Cleaner's gonna be around. So if you see one of them walking down the hall, try to go in the opposite direction, duck into the bathroom or the cafeteria, or if you have to walk by them, pretend you're blind and start feeling the wall as you go by. If you're at a desk and they come by, try to look busy. And whatever you do, *don't* invite them to play in the team Doom game. They can't play worth beans and are very sore losers.

Hopefully, you'll never have to confront the Section housekeeping staff. Just stick to the ones at the Hyatt. But if you do, just remember, a good cup of Irish Creme does wonders!

That's just one of the little hints we'll explore in chapter 11, Tips of the Trade.

CHAPTER 11

Tips of the Trade

By now you've realized that being a recruit in this outfit is no picnic. We've tried to give you as many hints as we could manage in each of the chapters, so I hope you were taking good notes. But we've also gathered a few additional tips and words of wisdom that we've included in this chapter to hopefully round out your training. So take heed and refer back here often.

Michael's tip for cauterizing a wound:

If you get shot behind enemy lines or left for dead by your team, you can cauterize a gunshot wound by yourself. Simply separate several bullet casings (two are good, three are better), and pour the gunpowder over the wound, taking care to cover the wound thoroughly. Then ignite the powder with a match or lighter. It'll hurt like hell, but the wound should close—if enough powder is used. Caution: Be careful not to use too much powder or you could blow your arm or leg off!

Walter's tips for using C4:

Since C4 comes in a wide variety of shapes and sizes, always check your tube of lipstick before twisting it open and applying. You'd hate to blow your lips off just for a bit of color! Also, if you happen to have a stick of red-and-green chewing gum, for heaven's sake, DON'T CHEW IT!!! This is our thin, Christmas version of C4 (or as some people call it, the "Red Light-Green Light" sticks) and can blow a door at ten paces or your mouth off at one! When in doubt, just assume it's C4 and use as such. That way, if the lipstick just smears, then it's just lipstick, or if the chewing gum just sticks to the wall looking stupid, then it's a good bet it's not C4. But better safe than sorry!

Birkoff's tips for hiding computer files:
Computer files can be easily hidden from prying eyes. Encryption routines are good but tedious and too slow to use on a mission. To quickly hide a file while on assignment, save it as a text file and label it "WINDOWS_95_INSTALL." No one in their right mind will open that file to take a look!

Also, never use a KL transform to run a location sim. The noise from running it sounds like someone beating on a drum a mile away! Only stupid people use this method, so you've been warned!

Timmy's tip for surviving being an RSO:
Don't wear anything *red* if you can help it! Try not to bump your head on the van walls and if anyone yells for backup: Don't go! That's a sure sign they need a body shield and you're it!

Eric's tip for tolerating surveillance:
First off, *always* wear clothing to bed! You never know who's watching! Also, the light under your stove isn't really a light; it's a camera. Same thing with the dirt splotch in the corner of the bathroom ceiling. It's not that we're really concerned with what you eat or whether you brush your teeth. It's just that those of us on watcher detail are *very* lonely! So just watch what you do at home cause we're sure watching you!

Madeline's tip for mentally torturing someone:
Find their weakness and exploit it! If they hate small spaces, put them in a box. If they're afraid of snakes, lock them in a room with a few. If

they're afraid of admitting their feelings about certain people and things, force them to work with them daily. If you don't want any information used against you, be strong and show no fear. NO FEAR gear is excellent for reinforcing that motto in your head. I wear it whenever I'm not in Section.

Nikita's general tips for surviving around here:
Never trust anyone here. They all lie at one time or another! Always wear sunglasses to a briefing. That way if you don't like what Ops is saying, you can roll your eyes in the back of your head and he'll never know. If you want a better gun, just wear a short skirt and low-cut shirt around Walter. Of course if you're a guy, that might look weird, but hey, whatever works! Also, be nice to Fred; he can either make you or break you around here.

Cherie's tips for successfully completing laser target training:
Start your shots in the upper left-hand corner of the room. The sim always begins from this position. When the ugly guy materializes, DUCK! Unless you're less than four feet tall, he'll hit you; and, geez, does that hurt!

(Yes, and finally a tip from yours truly)

Tel's tips for dealing with Michael and Madeline:
Never underestimate the power of Irish Creme coffee! It does wonders around here, For Madeline, never underestimate the power of chocolate! Yes, she's a closet chocoholic! But it has to be Godiva chocolates or she won't touch them! You know what impeccable taste she has.

Well, hopefully you'll be able to use these tips at one time or another before you die. Just kidding! As you can see, while we are very serious about what we do, we do have a sense of humor at times around here. Which brings us to our final chapter: What You're Allowed to Do for Fun.

CHAPTER 12

What You're Allowed to Do for Fun

If we've given you the impression throughout this book that life in Section is all work, and mostly tedious, it's not! Far from it, actually. There are lots of interesting things to do in the Section and plenty more outside of it.

With the recent loss of a great number of staff due to the Red Cell incident, and in an effort to boost morale around here, Ops has relaxed his stance on what we can do for fun in our downtime. So we have lots more options than we did a few months ago. Here's a list of some of our favorite things to do:

Shopping. This is a fun one! As an operative, you often have days with nothing to do, no one to kill, nothing to blow up. So to relieve the boredom, you're given credit cards up the wazoo with unlimited spending limits, and the best part is you don't have to pay it off. This is great when Macy's is having a white sale or you just can't resist buying that new car.

Team Quake playing. We're pretty ruthless when it comes to this game. We have individual competition (which Birkoff, of course, usually wins). But we also have team competition. Team 1 (Michael, Birkoff, Nikita, and Timmy) are pretty tough competition for the rest of us. Plus, Michael's a sore loser when he can't frag well. But this is what makes the team competition so interesting. You finally get a chance to irritate someone who in real life you'd be terrified of mouthing off to.

Wedging RSOs. OK, I know this is a cheap thrill; but hey, it's a thrill anyway! Just be careful not to do it too hard or you may have a dead RSO on your hands (literally!).

Going to the movies. Yes, we like to go to the movies whenever possible. We especially love the action films. It's really fun to sit there and make comments about all the stupid, idiotic things the hero is doing. It's usually so far removed from what we do in the Section, we usually laugh through the whole show and throw popcorn at the screen!

Eating out. Not one of my personal favorites, but some operatives really are gourmands. Since we have unlimited spending plastic (no, *not* plastique—don't get these two confused), for those that do love to eat, there are always plenty of first-class restaurants to try no matter where we are. Wait, I take that back. There have been a couple of times we've been in places where we'd have killed for a hamburger let alone going to a restaurant where the silverware isn't made of plastic (no, not plastique— how many times do I have to tell you not to confuse the two?). But for the food fanatics among us, this can certainly be a fun option!

Partying. We don't get the opportunity to do this one too often unless we're on assignment, but every so often one of us gets in the mood and throws a really good bash. Madeline is actually the best basher (oh, that came out wrong, didn't it?). Her parties tend to be really fun and filled with interesting mind games. Somehow though, it always seems that she's still testing us even when she swears it's just innocent fun. Walter throws a good bash, too. Kinda like a love-in from the sixties. It's fun to watch the younger recruits freak out at some of the stuff that goes on during one of these things.

Laser tag. We've actually been asked to leave QZAR several times for running up such a high score the computer couldn't track it. When about six to eight of us get really bored or are in a goofy mood, we'll head down there and take over the place late at night. Michael gives them one of his looks, and the place clears out! Two teams of Section operatives competing is fun to watch. Our accuracy is nearly perfect and the music makes it that much more fun (plus, it beats our laser-tag arena, where it *really* hurts when you get hit!). Michael and Timmy are great to have on your team. Michael doesn't even hide around the barricades, he just walks through the maze, gun in front of him, and shoots anything that moves. If he gets to your base, you're dead. He'll stand there and plug away till the base counter overloads. Timmy's a bit more animated. He gets into the Rambo-James Bond deal and ducks and rolls for cover, shooting from the floor most of the time. The referees try to kick him out, but he's usually too hard to catch. But this is loads of fun; so if you get the chance to play, I highly recommend it!

Playing practical jokes on operatives. You notice I didn't say Operations. He doesn't take kindly to practical jokes directed at him. Real party pooper. But the rest of us are more fun loving. Usually, for some reason, we pick an operative, and that week the unlucky soul is the brunt of all our practical jokes. The beginning of the week we start out easy. Things like a fly-in-the-ice-cube trick or punching holes in a cup to make it leak. But things get increasingly more interesting by the middle of the week. We removed all the furniture from Brian's office one time and deleted all Michael's files off his laptop another time (we did save them on a disk first, of course. We're not *that* mean!). But by the end of the week, look out! We've been known to replace live ammo with blanks and put superglue on the com units' earpieces. Birkoff really hated that one! Why do you think he keeps his hair short now? So, if it's your turn to be the brunt of the jokes this week, just remember, it's only for a week. How much harm could we possibly do in one measly week? (Don't answer that!)

Antagonizing the Coke guy and the Pepsi dude. This is sort of along the lines of playing practical jokes, but only with these guys. As I told you before, these two hate each other and it's really fun to play them off one another. You start by telling the Coke guy that you have decided that you really prefer Pepsi much better and are going to insist that the Pepsi dude be given ALL the Section's business from now on. This usually turns him a real pretty shade of red (the same color as on the Coke cans), and he storms off in a huff. Next, you go to the Pepsi dude and tell him that the last batch of Pepsi he delivered gave you hives and you think it would be best if the Section just had Coke from now on. He'll glare at you and try to argue with you about the merits of Pepsi. At this, you just wave your hand and shake your head and walk away. Just try not to giggle till you're out of sight or you'll blow the whole scene. We don't do this one too often, but every once in a while it's fun to stir these two up. I've actually seen them throw cans like hand grenades at each other after one of these little setups.

Posting pictures of Ops out on the Web (last but not least and probably our all-time favorite). What can be so fun about that? you ask. Well, we sort of change the pictures before we post them. Like giving Ops a third eye or an extra nose (or something coming out of his nose). Okay, so it's juvenile; but hey, it's very enjoyable! Remember those cameras in your apartment Eric told you about in the last chapter? Well we've installed some in Ops's home, too, you know! After all, if it's good enough for us, it's good enough for him, too! So next time you see pictures of Ops sitting in his underwear with a beer watching TV (probably football—he's a big 49ers fan!), those aren't faked—*they're real!!* But you didn't hear that from me!

So there you have it, gang: the complete *Idiot's Guide to Section One*! Hope you took good notes and found this information fun and, of course, informative. As I said in the beginning, Madeline will be quizzing you from time to time, as will Michael and myself, so make sure you refer back here often. As always, if you have any questions, drop me a note or yell it out to me next time we're on assignment together. Take care and live long and prosper (oh wait, wrong greeting!). Don't get dead. It's so permanent!

ACKNOWLEDGMENTS

This guide couldn't have been possible without the wonderful story lines and character portrayals from the cast of USA Network's original television production of *La Femme Nikita*. Thanks. We love Eugene, Alberta, Don, Matthew, Roy, and Peta! Keep up the wonderful job! To the crew of the show, thanks for your hard work on putting this on week after week you all! Thanks for making television fun to watch again!

Thanks to Chris Heyn for keeping the *LFN* list entertained for months with his witty comments. Hope to see more of you sometime soon!

And a special thanks to my kids, Brenton and Chris, for helping put this whole thing together, including comments, editing, and general snide remarks.

Hope you enjoyed reading it as much as we did putting it together!

LA ENCYCLOPEDIA NIKITA

SEASON ONE

A

AIMES, ROGER: An operative in Section One. He has an eight-year-old son, Kyle, about whom Section One doesn't know. When a criminal named Suba kidnaps the boy to force Roger to betray Section One, the agency soon finds out and has Roger killed to prevent any future compromises of their security. ["Treason"]

ANDY: An employee of Perry Bauer. To prove he has a deadly chemical, Bauer demonstrates it on Andy, killing the young man. ["Love"]

B

BAGGOT: An associate of Frederick Borsos. He negotiates to get the CM-12 chip from Steven Wolfe and the others. ["Missing"]

BAKUNIN: The favorite writer of the computer geek, J.B. ["Simone"]

BAUER, PERRY: A high-powered facilitator who helps to supply material to terrorist organizations such as Hamas, the IRA, and the Red Brigade. He kills his foster son, Andy, to prove to his terrorist clients that the chemical he has acquired is the real thing. His household is infiltrated by Michael and Nikita, who masquerade as the mercenary team of Peter and Sage. Although he is defeated and captured after being responsible for the deaths of innocent people, Section One has him come to work for them as a double agent. ["Love"]

BENKO, ILYA: A vicious terrorist who hates Section One. He captures Lange, one of Section One's operatives. When Benko loses the bidding to get the copy of the Section One directory from Harding, he kills Harding. In the end Benko is captured by Section One. ["Gray"]

BERRIS, RAYMOND: A member of the group of domestic terrorists known as the Glass Curtain. He meets with Nikita, who is masquerading as a contact named J.B. ["Simone"]

BILL: He and his friend Tim try to accost Lisa Fanning but she is saved by Michael. It was actually a setup by Section One to help make Lisa trust and depend on Michael more so that she'll listen to his requests to betray her husband. ["Obsessed"]

BIRKOFF: Computer specialist for Section One. He teaches Nikita how to get into computer files. ["Nikita"] Birkoff actually lives at Section One. Once when he's forced to use a gun to kill a man to save his own life, he has a difficult time coping because he's a computer expert, not an assassin. ["Noise"]

BOGGS: A government agent who works with Kiley. He is actually on the payroll of Suba and murders Kiley on the orders of Suba. ["Treason"]

BORSOS, FREDERICK: A terrorist. He wants to steal a CM-12 missile-guidance chip. His associate is Baggot. ["Missing"]

BRIAN: The Section One agent who trained Karyn. He is killed during a shoot-out in a nightclub, but his death is more than it seems. Karyn shot him. She claims that Brian had raped her many times during her training period. ["Recruit"]

BRIANNE: An agent of Section One they have held in abeyance because they believe she is unstable. ["Gambit"]

BRODA STATE HOSPITAL: Where Angie Georgiev works as a nurse. When Michael is left behind after a raid, he forces this woman to help him. ["Rescue"]

BRODSKY: A negotiator for those who want to buy the nuclear trigger from John and Helen Wicke. He's captured by Section One and tortured in order to discover whom he represents. ["Mother"]

BRUNER, ALEXEI: The son of Zoran Bruner and the brother of Maria Bruner. He is killed by Michael during the raid on the royal palace of Jovan Mijovich. ["Verdict"]

BRUNER, MARIA: The daughter of Zoran Bruner. She was raped when her village of Vakul was destroyed. The leader of the invasion force was Jovan Mijovich. ["Verdict"]

BRUNER, ZORAN: He and his comrades raid the inaugural ball of Jovan Mijovich and intend to execute him for crimes for which they believe him responsible. He is killed by Nikita when he tries to kill Jovan Mijovich. ["Verdict"]

C

CARLA: Nikita's next-door neighbor in the apartment building where she lives. ["Nikita"]

CASEY: The five-year-old daughter of Gray Wellman. ["Choice"]

CHANDLER, ALEC: A man Nikita saves from being killed by a hit-and-run driver. The accident was a setup so that Nikita could meet the man, who is wealthy and has a charity that supposedly helps street kids but actually sells them into slavery. At first Nikita knows only that he launders money for criminal organizations, using his charity as a front. He has links to the Russian mafia and the Triad. When he discovers that Nikita is a spy, he plans to sell her into slavery, too. When Section One moves in on him, Chandler tries to escape but is burned to death when his escape plan fails. ["Charity"]

CHUCK: An operative in Section One. He is killed when John Wicke activates a bomb he had delivered. ["Mother"]

CM-12: A state-of-the-art missile-guidance chip, which terrorist Frederick Borsos wants to steal. ["Missing"]

COSTAS: A thug who works for the terrorist Gabriel Tyler. ["Mercy"]

CRANE, JACK: A pervert who attacks Nikita in an alley. She brutally beats him. He's a killer who has raped and murdered eight women. Nikita can't testify against him without being exposed, so in the end she has to kill Crane. ["Voices"]

CRAWFORD: An operative in Section One. He's killed while trying to gain access to the palace where Jovan Mijovich is being held prisoner. ["Verdict"]

CROSS: An instructor in Section One. He is supervising an uncontrollable agent named Shellen. ["Gambit"]

D

DANIEL: An operative of Section One. He uses the cover name Dennis Larsen when he approaches Gray Wellman while looking for a secret computer disc. ["Gray"]

DARROW, JASON: A freelance arms dealer (but, then, aren't they all?). Though *he's* not anymore, because his body was found floating in the Mediterranean Sea. ["Brainwash"]

DAVENPORT, PAULA: A woman Walter was once involved with and whom he didn't want to lie to like all the others. ["Choice"]

DEAN, MARCO: One of a trio of men planning to steal the CM-12 missile-guidance chip. The other two men are Vincent Shirov and Steven Wolfe. ["Missing"]

DE ANZA BUILDING: The site of a test to be conducted of the nerve gas Elvira. ["Love"]

DEKKER: An underling who works for Suba. ["Treason"]

DELURE ELECTRONICS: Located in Chadwick, England. They build the brainwashing device known as a "Phasing Shell." Section One invades the plant. ["Brainwash"]

DOMINIC: A member of Red Cell who has declared war on Section One and ordered hits on all Section One agents. He captures Nikita and tortures her to get the location of the Section One substation. When Michael tries to rescue Nikita, he is also captured. They are both tortured. When they escape, Nikita kills Dominic in cold blood. ["War"]

DRAIZIN: An operative in Section One. He is assigned to trail the terrorist Gabriel Tyler. But Tyler spots Draizin and kills him. ["Mercy"]

E

ELDER, LEON: A terrorist who does business with an embassy official named Tossi. Elder is finally captured by Section One, but only after he kills Tossi. ["Voices"]

ELEGRA INDUSTRIES: A company in Ontario, Canada, that manufactures cobalt 60. It is infiltrated by the terrorist Gregor Kessler, who needs some cobalt 60 to perform a terrorist attack on an American city's water supply. ["Gambit"]

ELI: A thug who works for the terrorist Gabriel Tyler. ["Mercy"]

ELVIRA: A deadly VX-class chemical agent that combines chemically with KHS-05 to become a lethal nerve gas. ["Love"]

EMIL: One of the servants who work for John and Helen Wicke. ["Mother"]

F

FANNING, DAVID: A hit man. He has something called "The Book," which refers to a set of documents that could damage Western interests. No one can harm him until "The Book" is recovered from him. His wife is Lisa Fanning, and he demands perfection from her, commanding her to exercise and lose weight to please him. When Lisa goes out, he has his henchman Frank Thorn follow her. When Thorn sees Lisa with Michael, Section One has Thorn killed. Later Fanning is captured by Section One, interrogated, and then disposed of. ["Obsessed"]

FANNING, LISA: A thirty-year-old woman. The wife of hit man David Fanning. Nikita infiltrates her household by masquerading as a personal trainer. Lisa wants to lose weight to please her overly critical husband, fearing she will make him angry. Nikita introduces Lisa to Michael, who seduces her. But he's just using Lisa to get at her husband. When David is captured, Michael sees to it that Lisa gets a million dollars of her husband's money so that she'll never have to worry about anything ever again. ["Obsessed"]

FEIGER: The man who introduced Peter and Sage to each other in Frankfurt, Germany. He worked for Section One. ["Love"]

FENG: The new Chinese premiere, who is targeted for assassination by Mongolian extremists. Their tool of assassination is a brainwashing device they created called a "Phasing Shell." ["Brainwash"]

FIRESTEIN, DOCTOR: The cover name given to Rudy Haynes when Nikita takes him to the embassy ball to try to identify Maygar. ["Innocent"]

FIRESTEIN, JOAN: The cover name used by Nikita for an embassy ball where Section One is trying to identify a man involved in a nuclear warhead smuggling plot. ["Innocent"]

FRANKEL, MAJOR: An officer in the police force of the European country where Michael has been left behind after a raid by Section One. He works for Colonel Petrosian. ["Rescue"]

FRAYN, DETECTIVE: A cover name used by Madeline when interviewing passengers from the bus Harding rode when he slipped the secret computer disc to someone. ["Gray"]

FREEMAN, MARK: He delivers the nuclear trigger to John and Helen Wicke. John Wicke has his limo driver assassinate Freeman to cover their tracks. ["Mother"]

G

GAIL: An operative in Section One. ["Noise"]

GAINES, ANNIE: Although she's never met him, her father is Norris Gaines, aka Gregor Kessler. She is a foreign exchange student attending university in Norway. Section One brings Annie in to use her in order to get her father to reveal information to them. Instead, he kills his own daughter when she gets close to him. He had believed that Section One was going to torture her, but he was wrong and killed his own daughter unnecessarily. ["Gambit"]

GAINES, NORRIS: The real name of terrorist Gregor Kessler, Gaines was born in Germany in 1946 to Polish immigrants. His parents were murdered in 1952 by an anti-immigrant hate group. For the next eight years he lived in a state-run orphanage. At age fourteen he murdered two fellow students and then escaped from the facility. Eleven years later he resurfaced under the name Gregor Kessler. He had a daughter named Annie, whom he secretly supported but had never met. ["Gambit"]

GANZ, DOCTOR: A doctor who works in the Broda State Hospital in the Eastern European country where Section One destroyed a weapons plant. ["Rescue"]

GARSHA: A man who brokers assassins. He has been given the contract by Red Cell to take out Section One. He is located in Rabat, Morocco. ["War"]

GEORGE: The name of a servant who works for Alec Chandler. ["Charity"]

GEORGIEV, ANGIE: A nurse at the Broda State Hospital. Michael forces her to help him when he's left behind after a raid, but because she hates the government of her country, she is more than willing to assist him. Government operatives figure out that she's helping Michael and track her down. She sacrifices herself to help Michael escape. ["Rescue"]

GLASS CURTAIN: A terrorist group that practices the politics of chaos and destruction. They have something that can alter patterns on the radar screens of air-traffic control and thereby cause planes to collide. Group members are highly skilled and intelligent. The Glass Curtain is destroyed when their former prisoner, Simone, kills its leader and herself. ["Simone"]

GOLDEN, R. J.: A man being stalked by Section One. He's captured with the help of Nikita. He's an arms supplier for Cyrus Kavali, whom Section One wants to find to prevent his return to power. ["Noise"]

GRAYSTONE: A password used to get into the computer files of Alec Chandler. ["Charity"]

GRIFFIN: An assassin who has been hired to kill Jovan Mijovich. Griffin also killed the person who passed along information on him to Michael. Griffin turns out to be a woman. ["Verdict"]

H

HARDIN: One of the business associates of Alec Chandler. ["Charity"]

HARDING: He breaks into the Section One computer and downloads a copy of the directory. He agrees to auction the directory off to the highest bidder, forcing Section One to bid against Ilya Benko, one of Section One's greatest enemies. Harding makes a deal with Section One, but when he's on his way to deliver the disc, he detects that he's being followed. While on a bus, Harding hides the disc on an unsuspecting passenger, who must be found by Section One before Benko, who assassinates Harding, finds him and the disc. ["Gray"]

HARRY: A contact Nikita meets in a cafe. ["Friend"]

HAYES, JULIAN: Project leader at Elegra Industries. He is murdered by Gregor Kessler, who surgically removes one of Hayes's eyes in order to use a retina scan to enter a vault containing cobalt 60. ["Gambit"]

HAYNES, BELINDA: The retarded sister of Rudy Haynes. ["Innocent"]

HAYNES, RUDY: A pizza delivery man. Early thirties. He gets involved with a plot to smuggle a nuclear warhead into the U.S. when he sees the truck transporting the device, the man with the trigger, and the body of a dead airplane crewman. He has a sister with Down's syndrome. He is captured and interrogated by Section One because they think he's involved in the bomb plot. ["Innocent"]

HESTER: He has perfected a program which can interfere with an aircraft's radar. ["Simone"]

HEZBOLLAH: An anti-West terrorist group entering into an alliance with other terrorist organizations. The alliance is being brokered by Gideon Van Vactor. ["Nikita"]

J

JACKSON, DELRAY: A police detective investigating the beating of the pervert named Jack Crane who attacked Nikita. ["Voices"]

J.B.: A computer geek who knows how to contact the group of domestic terrorists known as the Glass Curtain. He is interrogated by Section One and impersonated by Nikita. ["Simone"]

JENNEL: A buyer in a drug deal. He's killed when he's ripped off by Rosewood, a CIA antidrug interdiction force. ["Choice"]

JOSEPHINE: The code name Nikita is given when she joins Section One. ["Nikita"]

K

KARYN: A recruit whom Nikita has to judge as to whether she's qualified to serve Section One. Her previous instructor, Brian, was afraid of Karyn and believed her to be psychotic. Karyn liked to kill, and in fact, at age seven had killed her own grandmother. Karyn likes being in Section One because she gets a thrill out of killing. Operations decides that Karyn is too unstable and cancels her. Nikita had independently come to the same conclusion. ["Recruit"]

KASSAR: Lebanese. Involved in a plot to smuggle a nuclear warhead into the United States. He sends a transmission notifying Section One of the bomb and then commits suicide. ["Innocent"]

KAVALI, CYRUS: A man Section One wants to find. They pull in a man named Golden to get information on Kavali's whereabouts. He's the deposed head of a nation. This former dictator wants to regain his lost power. ["Noise"]

KENNY: He works for Alec Chandler and discovers a listening device that Nikita had planted on the hull of his yacht. ["Charity"]

KESSLER, GREGOR: A terrorist who is a master of disguise. He infiltrates Elegra Industries and steals some cobalt 60, which his comrades can use to carry out a terrorist attack. His real name is Norris Gaines. He has a daughter by a woman who died in childbirth in the early 1980s. ["Gambit"]

KEVIN: Carla's new boyfriend, but he's not really interested in her. He makes the mistake of coming on to Nikita. ["Voices"]

KILEY: A government agent who warns Suba to leave the country because they won't protect him anymore. ["Treason"]

KLODNO PETROCHEMICAL PLANT: Located in Central Europe, it is actually a weapons plant. It is attacked by the forces of

Section One. While their target is destroyed, Michael is injured and then left behind. ["Rescue"]

KOI: An agent in Section One. ["Simone"]

KOSTEN: The assistant to Alec Chandler. He's framed by Michael to appear to betray Chandler, who then gets rid of him. ["Charity"]

KOUSSAKIS: A wedding party where David Fanning assassinates two people. ["Obsessed"]

KREIZEL, ANDRE: Stole a letter containing a NATO scenario for assassinating Moslem officials. He wants fifty million dollars to keep him from releasing the document. Nikita, Michael, and Karyn are sent to track him down and retrieve the letter. They succeed. Karyn even saves Nikita's life when Nikita's gun runs out of ammo and Kreizel is about to shoot Nikita. Karyn shoots and kills Kreizel, instead. ["Recruit"]

KYLE: An eight-year-old boy. He is Roger Aimes's son. The boy has been kidnapped by Suba and is being held hostage to force Roger Aimes to inform on Section One for Suba. ["Treason"]

L

LANGE: An operative of Section One who is captured and turned over to Ilya Benko, one of the most vicious terrorists around. Benko murders and beheads Lange. ["Gray"]

LEGION: A terrorist group responsible for the bombing of the World Games and three airline crashes. ["Friend"]

LEWIS, DETECTIVE: Arrives at the home of Helen Wicke to inform her that John Wicke was killed in a car accident. Actually Wicke was assassinated and this is just a cover story. ["Mother"]

LINA: An Asian woman who is a terrorist buying the nerve gas Elvira from Perry Bauer. ["Love"]

LOLLAR: An associate of hit man David Fanning. He's killed by Nikita when Section One raids Fanning's home. ["Obsessed"]

LONNIE: An operative of Section One. He is working on the team planning to trace Cyrus Kavali by tagging a shipment of missiles ready to be secretly sent to him. He's murdered by someone else who has an art gallery under surveillance. ["Noise"]

M

MADELINE: One of Nikita's superiors at Section One. Nikita meets Madeline the first day of her arrival at the covert operations center. Madeline teaches Nikita how to enhance her feminine attributes. ["Nikita"] Little is known about Madeline until a terrorist Section One captures, named Gregor Kessler, reveals that he knows quite a lot about Madeline, including that she had a sister who died when Madeline was very young, a revelation that unnerves Madeline a great deal. ["Gambit"]

MAYGAR, GUY: Lebanese. Involved in a plot to smuggle a nuclear warhead into the United States. He is captured by Section One and tortured (one of his fingers is cut off) to get the information on the bomb. ["Innocent"]

MEL: A police ballistics assistant at the crime scene where Jack Crane attacked Nikita. ["Voices"]

MICHAEL: The first person Nikita meets when she is recruited from prison to become a trained assassin for Section One. Michael is her instructor. ["Nikita"] Michael becomes interested in Nikita on a more-than-professional level and even covers for her, thereby saving her life. We later learn that he had a lover who he'd believed was dead; but actually she'd been captured by the enemy and imprisoned for a few years. When freed, she takes revenge on her captors and then kills herself. ["Simone"] It is later revealed that Michael and Simone had a son who'd died in infancy. ["War"]

MIJOVICH, JOVAN: A diplomat who is working to restore peace between opposing factions and has been marked for death by terrorists because he is responsible for the execution of two Legion terrorists. He is placed under the protection of Section One. ["Friend"] Newly elected premiere of a nation friendly to the West. Section One once again moves in to protect him from assassination, this time from an assassin named Griffin. Griffin is killed, but the real threat is a man named Bruner, who takes Mijovich prisoner. Zoran Bruner accuses Jovan Mijovich of rape and murder, but Nikita doesn't believe it's possible. Ultimately he is saved by Nikita, who kills Zoran Bruner. Then Nikita discovers that Bruner had been right all along. ["Verdict"]

MOONEY: The pilot of a plane that crashes because an air traffic controller was fed incorrect data on his radar. ["Simone"]

MORRISON: An agent of Section One. ["Simone"]

N

NSA: National Security Agency. A covert investigating arm of the U.S. government devoted to protecting from terrorist incursions the domestic tranquillity of the United States.

O

O'BRIEN, MARCO: A police detective investigating the beating of the pervert, Jack Crane, who attacked Nikita. Marco gets a police artist to provide a sketch of Nikita and then tracks her down to her apartment, where he manages to get her fingerprints. He then learns who she really is. Nikita tells him to lose his intel on her and in exchange she'll kill Jack Crane. O'Brien refuses. In the end they frame O'Brien for Crane's murder and force him to either join Section One or be sent to prison for murder. ["Voices"]

OPERATIONS: The code name of the man who directs the covert activities of Section One. ["Nikita"]

ORNETT: An employee of arms dealer Perry Bauer. ["Love"]

P

PARKS, CHAN: An Asian technician who works at Delure Electronics. When confronted by Michael, Parks attracts the attention of guards, but in the gunfight that ensues, Parks is shot. She lives, however, and Michael kidnaps her to take back with him to Section One in the United States. ["Brainwash"]

PAUL: The name of a sentry who was guarding the home of Jerico Perez the night he was taken captive by Section One. ["Escape"]

PEREZ, CASSIAN: Spokesman for the terrorist group Tiburon. He has taken hostages to trade for associates arrested months earlier by his government. The only problem is that his associates are already dead, although he doesn't know that. When his brother is kidnapped, he refuses to give in and kills one of his hostages. He's later killed by Nikita when she rescues the remaining hostage. ["Escape"]

PEREZ, JERICO: The brother of terrorist leader Cassian Perez. When Section One moves in to kidnap him to get at Cassian, a firefight erupts and Jerico accidentally kills his own wife. ["Escape"]

PEREZ, SUZANNE: Wife of Jerico Perez, and sister-in-law of terrorist leader Cassian Perez. ["Escape"]

PETER: A professional European mercenary, part of a husband-and-wife team. His wife is Sage. Married for two years, they met through a German named Feiger. He and his wife are captured for interrogation by Section One and are replaced by Michael and Nikita. ["Love"]

PETROSIAN, COLONEL EGRAN: An officer in the police force of the European country where Michael has been left behind after a raid by Section One. He figures out where Michael must be and who has been helping him. Petrosian's assistant is Major Frankel. Petrosian actually works for Section One and has been a deep-cover agent for seventeen years. He fakes his death at the time Michael escapes so that he can flee the country. ["Rescue"]

PHASING SHELL: A virtual reality device that can be used for brainwashing. Nikita tests it to discover what information it conveys to its subject, and in the process she is secretly programmed to assassinate the same target Coleman Reilly would have taken out had he not killed himself. ["Brainwash"]

PORTER: An operative of Section One who is assassinated. His body is dumped in the canal off Broad Street. ["Gray"]

PRICE, OLIVER: Part of a CIA antidrug interdiction force called Rosewood. He helps to set up Ramone and Jennel to steal their drugs and money and to cover his involvement in the theft he kills Ray, the inside man. ["Choice"]

PRUITT DISTRIBUTORS: The cover name used by the Rosewood Group. ["Choice"]

R

RAMONE: A drug dealer who is killed when he's ripped off by Rosewood, a CIA antidrug interdiction force. ["Choice"]

RANDY: Head of security for the Wicke household. ["Mother"]

RAVE CLUB: An open club for computer geeks. Michael and Nikita find a contact there that can lead them to the Glass Curtain. ["Simone"]

RAVIC: One of Suba's guards. Nikita knocks him out while going to rescue Kyle. ["Treason"]

RAY: Helps set up Ramone, who realizes it and shoots Ray, precipitating a melee. ["Choice"]

RED CELL: A group that launches a war against Section One. A three-man hit squad goes after Nikita, but she takes them out. Red Cell is finally lured into an ambush and destroyed, but at great cost to Section One. ["War"]

REILLY, COLEMAN: A name found on a list taken from the body of arms dealer Jason Darrow. When Nikita mentions the name Jason Darrow to him, Reilly commits suicide. In his apartment they find a virtual reality device known as a "Phasing Shell." ["Brainwash"]

ROARK, JULIE: A woman who formerly knew Nikita. But the fact that she recognizes her (Nikita is, after all, supposed to have died in prison) creates jeopardy for all involved. Julie is a childhood friend, having attended Monroe Elementary school with Nikita. She turns out to be a terrorist who killed the real Julie Roark and took her place in order to get close to Nikita. Finally Nikita is forced to kill her. ["Friend"]

ROCHE, DOCTOR: A doctor who works in the Broda State Hospital in the Eastern European country where Section One destroyed a weapons plant. ["Rescue"]

ROSEWOOD: The code name for a CIA operation aimed at interfering with heroin distribution. ["Choice"]

ROSS, CHARLIE: A private detective who has been searching for the long-lost daughter of Helen Wicke. Her child was taken from her when she was in prison, and Ross believes that Nikita is that child. ["Mother"]

S

SAGE: A European, she is part of a husband-and-wife professional mercenary team. Her husband is Peter. Married for two years, they met through a German named Feiger. She and her husband are captured for interrogation by Section One and are replaced by Nikita and Michael. ["Love"]

SAUVAGE: The undersecretary in Paris. ["Innocent"]

SECTION ONE: The covert operations group that works outside the law to halve the activities of supercriminals and terrorists who have remained out of reach of normal police agencies. Nikita was taken from prison and forced to become a trained assassin and operative for Section One. Her training lasts two years. ["Nikita"]

SHAW, JOHNNY: A CIA agent contacted by Marco after he gets Nikita's fingerprints. ["Voices"]

SHAYS, STANLEY: A friend of Richard J. Spidel. Shays is a chemist who has developed a powerful, undetectable explosive, five ounces of which could level a building. Tyler wants the secret of the explosive Shays has developed and kidnaps him from the custody of the NSA. Shays is killed by Tyler when Nikita tries to rescue him. ["Mercy"]

SHELLEN: An agent of Section One they have recalled and not used in the field since he made grave errors on a mission in Budapest. He is considered to be uncontrollably aggressive. He is used to interrogate Kessler because they know that Kessler will kill the man, disguise himself as Shellen, and escape, enabling them to follow him. ["Gambit"]

SHINING PATH: An anti-West terrorist group entering into an alliance with other terrorist organizations. The alliance is being brokered by Gideon Van Victor. ["Nikita"]

SHIROV, VINCENT: One of a trio of men planning to steal the CM-12 missile-guidance chip. The other two men are Marco Dean and Steven Wolfe. ["Missing"]

SIMONE: She was Michael's wife until she was killed by the Glass Curtain, or at least he believes she was killed. Actually she was captured and kept prisoner for three years. When she is freed by Michael and Nikita, Simone decides that after what she's been through, all she has left is to get revenge on the Glass Curtain by destroying it and Errol Sparks, and herself as well. ["Simone"]

SIO BHAN: A cyberpunk friend of Errol Sparks. ["Simone"]

SKYLER: Acts as middleman between Hardin and Chandler. ["Charity"]

SOLTIS: A terrorist in the Legion who kidnaps and interrogates Nikita as to the whereabouts of Jovan Mijovich. ["Friend"]

SPARKS, ERROL: A disaffected anarchist who runs the terrorist organization the Glass Curtain. He is killed by Simone. ["Simone"]

SPIDEL, RICHARD J.: In his late twenties. An associate of the terrorist named Tyler, yet he has no known criminal ties and seems to be an honest businessman who's never been in trouble. He knows a chemist named Stanley Shays; and Tyler wants the secret of the explosive Shays has developed. Spidel is taken in for questioning by the NSA, but he and the NSA agents are all assassinated; and Stanley Shays is kidnapped by Tyler. ["Mercy"]

STAN: An operative in Section One who has been there for fourteen years. ["Nikita"]

STEPHANIE: The girlfriend of Perry Bauer. ["Love"]

STOKES: The real killer whose crime Nikita was convicted of. She had encountered and struggled with the killer and wrestled the knife away from him, but the police found Nikita standing over the body of the man Stokes had murdered—and she was holding the bloody knife. ["Nikita"]

STOPPEL, MICK: A contact for terrorist Ilya Benko. ["Gray"]

SUBA: A middle-aged criminal who has been in the employ of the U.S. government trying to obtain waste uranium from power plants. They choose to terminate their working relationship when Suba becomes a liability. Section One is ordered to deport him because The Agency (CIA?) has been compromised. Since his weakness is tall blondes, Nikita is chosen to infiltrate his inner circle. ["Treason"]

SUBSTATION: The secret retreat center for Section One when they are under attack. It is located in the subbasement of the abandoned rendering plant, or so Nikita is told. Actually, this is a trap to lure the Red Cell members to come after them, where the terrorists are killed in an ambush. ["War"]

T

TED: An operative in Section One working with Nikita on the Rosewood matter. ["Choice"]

TERRY: A business associate of Alec Chandler who pays him for the latest group of children he's selling into slavery. ["Charity"]

THORN, FRANK: The right-hand man of hit man David Fanning. He follows Lisa when she and Nikita go jogging. When Thorn sees Lisa with Michael, Section One has him killed before he can report back to Fanning. ["Obsessed"]

TIBURON: The name of a terrorist group in South America. Their spokesman is Cassian Perez. They abduct two marine guards from in front of an embassy to hold them hostage. One of the marines is killed when Suzanne Perez dies during the abduction of Jerico Perez. ["Escape"]

TIKO: A terrorist in the Legion who kidnaps and interrogates Nikita as to the whereabouts of Jovan Mijovich. ["Friend"]

TIM: He and his friend Bill try to accost Lisa Fanning, but she is saved by Michael. It was actually a setup by Section One to help make Lisa trust and depend on Michael so that she'll listen to his requests to betray her husband. ["Obsessed"]

TOSSI: An embassy official who is under the surveillance of Section One. One morning when he goes jogging, he is kidnapped by Section One and forced to reveal how to contact terrorist Leon Elder. The meeting goes badly and Tossi is killed by Elder. ["Voices"]

LA ENCYCLOPEDIA NIKITA

TOWNSEND, ANDREW: A lance corporal in the marines who is taken hostage by the terrorist group Tiburon. ["Escape"]

TYLER, GABRIEL: A European terrorist being stalked by Section One. He is a high-ranking member of the Freedom League, an extremist group trying to gain control in the Balkans. Tyler wants the secret of the new explosive Stanley Shays has developed, and Richard J. Spidel wants to sell it to him. Tyler ultimately kills Spidel and kidnaps Shays. Tyler is killed by Nikita when she tries to rescue Shays. ["Mercy"]

U

UNITED COALITION: A terrorist group who has threatened to contaminate with cobalt 60 the water supply of a major city. They hire the notorious terrorist Gregor Kessler to carry out their threat. ["Gambit"]

V

VACTOR, GIDEON VAN: He is brokering an alliance between anti-West terrorist groups. ["Nikita"]

VAKUL: A village supposedly destroyed by the forces of Jovan Mijovich. Zoran Bruner is from that village and he intends to exact revenge for its destruction. Zoran's daughter, Maria, was raped during the attack by Jovan Mijovich. ["Verdict"]

VALERY: A drug dealer working with Oliver Price. Valery is captured by Section One for interrogation and he reveals how to contact Price. ["Choice"]

156

LA ENCYCLOPEDIA NIKITA

W

WALLEN: The negotiator for arms dealers Helen and John Wicke. ["Mother"]

WALTER: One of Nikita's instructors in Section One. ["Nikita"]

WEBBER, ERIC: A member of Section One who offers to help Nikita escape. His plan seems foolproof and involves erasing all information about himself from the Section One computer files so that they cannot track his movements after he flees. Initially Nikita doesn't believe him and thinks that he's part of a trick being played on her by Section One to test her loyalty. Ultimately she decides not to escape with him, and it turns out that Section One was aware of Eric's plan all along. ["Escape"]

WELLMAN, GRAY: A passenger on a bus to whom Harding secretly slipped a computer disc. Harding expected to contact Gray later, but when Harding is killed, it becomes a race between Section One and terrorist Ilya Benko to find this passenger with the disc. Gray is an architect, and Nikita gets to know him in order to manipulate Benko into coming out from hiding to obtain the disc. Gray was once married to a woman name Chris, who died. He has a daughter named Casey. Nikita gets involved with him for a time but is forced by Section One to break off her relationship with him. ["Gray"]

WICKE, HELEN: An arms merchant married to John Wicke. Having dealt in arms since 1984, she and her husband come into possession of a nuclear trigger. She thinks that Nikita is her long-lost child; but then that's what she's *supposed* to think. ["Mother"]

WICKE, JOHN: An arms merchant since 1984, married to Helen Wicke. He and his wife come into possession of a nuclear trigger. When he discovers that Nikita is a phony, she kills him. ["Mother"]

WILLETTE, MRS.: Nikita's fourth-grade teacher at Monroe Elementary school. ["Friend"]

WINTERS, JANET: The hostess of an embassy ball. ["Innocent"]

WOLFE, STEVEN: The son of Operations. Operations asks Nikita to watch out for him on a mission, but he is actually trying to steal the CM-12 missile-guidance chip. His two cohorts are Marco Dean and Vincent Shirov. Steven believes that his father was kept as a prisoner of war in Vietnam and doesn't know that his father is Operations, the head of Section One. Operations wants his identity kept a secret. ["Missing"]

Y

YERKOVICH, JAY: A businessman Nikita goes up to in a bar. ["Noise"]

Z

ZYLAR CORPORATION: The company that developed the CM-12 missile-guidance chip. ["Missing"]

LA RESOURCES
NIKITA

EPISODE GUIDES

Cody's *LFN* Episode Guide
http://cherokee.simplenet.com/shows.htm

SOFCOM's *LFN* Episode Index
http://www.sofcom.com.au:80/tv/lammens/lafemme.htm

Baogin's Episode Index
http://www.geocities.com/TelevisionCity/4163/EPISODE_INDEX.html

La Femme Nikita Spoiler Index
http://hubcap.clemson.edu/~jmmyers/spoilers/spoilers.html

LJC's *La Femme Nikita* Page—Episode Guides
http://www.geocities.com/TelevisionCity/5235/epguide.html

NEWSGROUPS

alt.fan.la-femme.nikita

alt.fan.lafemme-nikita

MAILING LISTS

LFN Mailing List
Section2-Request@Listservice.net
(Send e-mail with the word *subscribe* in the body of the message)

LFN Mailing List Digest
Section2-Digest-Request@Listservice.net
(Send e-mail with the word *subscribe* in the body of the message)

LFN Mailing List Homepage
http://cherokee.simplenet.com/lfnlist.htm

LFN Mailing List Archive
http://www.geocities.com/TelevisionCity/Set/1281/

LFN FanFic Mailing List
majordomo@raven.me.fau.edu
(Send e-mail with the words *subscribe lfnfic-l* in the body of the message)

Royettes Mailing List
Royettes-request@cuenet.com
(Send e-mail with the word *subscribe* in the body of the message)

Royettes Mailing List Digest
Royettes-digest-request@cuenet.com
(Send e-mail with the word *subscribe* in the body of the message)

Birkoff Mailing List
birkoffbabes-request@userhome.com
(Send e-mail with the word *subscribe* in the subject line)

La Femme Nikita NewsLetter
http://www.geocities.com/TelevisionCity/4982/index.html

Chat Post
http://members.icanect.net/~duggal/LFN_Chat/chat_post.html

"The Operatives" Material Discussion List
nikita-request@listservice.net
(Send e-mail with the word *subscribe* in the body of the message)

"The Operatives" Material Discussion List Digest Mode
nikita-digest-request@listservice.net
(Send e-mail with the word *subscribe* in the body of the message)

FREQUENTLY ASKED QUESTIONS (FAQS)

LFN Spy Central
http://cherokee.simplenet.com/codename.htm

La Website Nikita
http://www.croushorn.com/nikita/index.html

USA Network's *La Femme Nikita* Homepage
http://www.usanetwork.com/content/backlot/nikita/nikita.html

Warner Bros. *La Femme Nikita* Page
http://www.virtuallot.com/cmp/action/ac04.htm

LA RESOURCES NIKITA

Michelle's *La Femme Nikita* Page
http://falcon.cs.mercer.edu:80/~wrenn_m/nikita.html

Tierrany's *La Femme Nikita* Homepage
http://www.geocities.com/TelevisionCity/9450/

Baoqin's *La Femme Nikita* Page
http://www.geocities.com/TelevisionCity/4163/

Simmie's *La Femme Nikita* Page
http://www.geocities.com/TelevisionCity/9489/

LJC's *La Femme Nikita* Page
http://www.geocities.com/TelevisionCity/5235/

KjunKutie's *LFN* Page
http://www.geocities.com/BourbonStreet/Delta/1963/lfn.htm

Section One
http://www.fortunecity.com/lavendar/rampling/1/

Layne's *LFN* Page
http://www.geocities.com/Hollywood/Lot/4591/

Codename: Katherine
http://www.geocities.com/TelevisionCity/5581/

LFN EyeCandy
http://www.geocities.com/TelevisionCity/Set/6820/

*La Femme Nikita…*The Series
http://www.vci.net/~susanhar/lfn/

Quinn's Page of *LFN* and Roy Dupuis Images
http://www.geocities.com/TelevisionCity/Set/7602/

Section One Database
http://lfn.mit.edu/lfn/

FAN FICTION WEBSITES

LFN FanFic Mailing List Homepage
http://www.geocities.com/TelevisionCity/Set/2487/

La Femme Nikita Fan Fiction
http://www.geocities.com/TelevisionCity/5932/index.html

KFFIC-L Fanfiction Homepage
http://cadserv.cadlab.vt.edu/kffic-l/

LJC's La Femme Nikita Page - Fan Fiction
http://www.geocities.com/TelevisionCity/5235/fanfic.html

SECTION TWO

Section Two's Homepage
http://cherokee.simplenet.com/codename.htm

Section Two Heads
http://members.tripod.com/~Gillinia/S2heads.htm

Lavender's *LFN* Page!
http://members.tripod.com/~Semca/index.html

Torquil's Mini *LFN* Page for Michael and Nikita
http://members.tripod.com/~Gillinia/S2heads.htm

Codename Lana
http://members.tripod.com/~Codename_Lana/

Section 2 *LFN* Web Ring
http://www.geocities.com/Area51/Zone/6738/ring.html

PETA WILSON

Peta Wilson Online
http://www.opni.com/~rowena/

La Femme Nikita Tribute
http://www.ripon.edu/students/spragueb/nikita.htm

ROY DUPUIS

Cody's Page for Roy
http://cherokee.simplenet.com/roy.htm

Michael's Operatives
http://www.logomancy.simplenet.com/SIDEKICKS/michael.html

Les Ombres De Michel
http://www.geocities.com/Paris/Metro/6085/

MATTHEW FERGUSON

Bruyere's Matthew Ferguson Page
http://www.geocities.com/Area51/Zone/6738/birkoff.html

Matthew Ferguson as Kane
http://www.spe.sony.com/Pictures/SonyClassics/remains/cast/ferguson.html

EUGENE ROBERT GLAZER

BlueGloJo's Page for Operations
http://members.aol.com/BlueGloJo/index.html

DON FRANCKS

Don Francks, in Profile
http://www.nextlevel.com/fantastic/p2.htm

NIGEL BENNETT

Nigel Bennett Index Page
http://www.erinet.com/nbfc/

Nigel Bennett Fan Club
http://www.erinet.com/nbfc/fanclub.htm

LUC BESSON

Books about Luc Besson's Movies
http://www.ifi.uio.no/~mariuswi/besson/misc/books.html

Luc Besson Films WWW Page
http://www.ifi.uio.no/~mariuswi/besson/index.html

Petit Hommage ‡ Luc Besson
http://w3.nationalnet.com/~berube/besson.htm
(French Luc Besson Homepage)

LFN ARTWORK

Mark's *LFN* Page
http://members.icanect.net/~tacke/lfn.html

La Website Nikita Art Page
http://www.croushorn.com/nikita/index.html

LJC's *La Femme Nikita* Page - Fanart
http://www.geocities.com/TelevisionCity/5235/fanart.html

ARTICLES

Femme Fatal
http://tripled.com/TVPLUS/Nikita.htm

Article Index
http://www.geocities.com/TelevisionCity/1045/articles.html

Chicago Sun-Times Review of *LFN* by Roger Ebert
http://www.suntimes.com/ebert/ebert_reviews/1991/04/642846.html

LJC's *La Femme Nikita* Page—Articles
http://www.geocities.com/TelevisionCity/5235/articles.html

CHAT SITES

The Official *LFN* Chat ;) Homepage
http://members.icanect.net/~duggal/LFN_Chat/

La Femme Nikita Chat Room
http://www.uidaho.edu/~dale9532/links/personal/chat.html

TV Guide's Peta Wilson Bulletin Board
http://www.tvguide.com/bbs/transcripts/peta.htm

TV Guide's *La Femme Nikita* Bulletin Board
http://bbs2.iguide.com:8086/television/peta/

MUSIC-RELATED SITES

Larold's Web Site
http://home.earthlink.net/~larold/index.html

Cusmus' *La Femme Nikita* Musique
http://members.aol.com/Cusmus/index.html

LFN SITE LISTS

Yahoo *LFN* Links
http://www.yahoo.com/News_and_Media/Television/Shows/Action/Femme_Nikita_La/

LFN Index
http://hubcap.clemson.edu/~jmmyers/lafemme.html

CGS Success Systems *La Femme Nikita* Sites
http://infoweb.magi.com/~datakes/lafemmen.htm

MISCELLANEOUS

The Directory
http://www.geocities.com/TelevisionCity/3243/

Sounds of *La Femme Nikita*
http://www.geocities.com/TelevisionCity/Set/2055/

Ryan's *LFN* Web Page
http://www.geocities.com/TelevisionCity/5287/

Blue Pirate's *La Femme Nikita*
http://members.aol.com/BluePirate/Nikita.html

MysticGirl's Page O'Stuff
http://www.geocities.com/TelevisionCity/Set/1435/

Robin's Miscellaneous Page
http://www.fwb.gulf.net/~robhorne/miscell.htm

Thracian's Autograph Page
http://members.tripod.com/~Thrac/autograph-index.html

Virtually Northwest story on the renewal
http://www.virtuallynw.com/~vnw/stories/1997/May/12/S229849.htm

jgdlittleb's *La Femme Nikita*
http://members.aol.com/jgdlittleb/nik/index.htm

Aradia's Nikita Page
http://www.dct.com/~aradia/nikita.html

Tiffany's *La Femme Nikita* Page
http://www.iinet.com/users/tvalley/Nikita.html

Issy's *LFN* Page
http://www.geocities.com/TelevisionCity/9513/index.html

Nikita & Section Operatives
http://www.bee.net/nibbles1/nikita.html

Psychological Profiles
http://www.geocities.com/Hollywood/8283/psychprof.html

La Femme Nikita Trivia Stories
http://www.geocities.com/TelevisionCity/4982/tstories.html

LA RESOURCES NIKITA

Trivia for *La Femme Nikita*
http://www.geocities.com/TelevisionCity/4982/trivia.html

The Basics
http://members.tripod.com/~Serina_Sec2/

Hedda's Hideaway
http://www.geocities.com/Area51/Zone/6738/home.html

Polly's *LFN* WebPage
http://www.angelfire.com/co/pollyrms/

Kelli's *LFN* Page
http://www.geocities.com/TelevisionCity/Set/2366/

La Femme Nikita Worship Page
http://members.tripod.com/~LA_FEMME_NIKITA_FAN/

Nikita
http://members.tripod.com/~Dimera/nikitafq.html

Karen's *LFN* Page
http://members.tripod.com/~la_femme_nikita/index-2.html

L'Espirit D'Amour
http://www.geocities.com/Hollywood/Academy/5723/

Beth's *La Femme Nikita* Page
http://www.geocities.com/TelevisionCity/Set/4254/

LFN Pictures
http://www.geocities.com/TelevisionCity/Set/4752/

ENTERTAINMENT RELATED SITES

TV Series Web Site
http://www.total.net/~delacote/tv.htm
(Part French and English)

Movie and TV Show Listing
http://users.aol.com/NTaylor333/movies.htm

CGS Success Systems TV Programs Sites
http://www.cgstv.com/index.html

ZENtertainment
http://www.zentertainment.com/

Ultimate TV Listing
http://www.ultimatetv.com

Washington Post Online TV Grids
http://www.tvhost.com/tvhost/guide/custom/washpost

TV Guide Online
http://www.tvguide.com/

JAM! Entertainment
http://www2.canoe.ca/Jam/home.html

Yahoo! Internet Life
http://www.yil.com/

TV Hebdo—Internet Edition
http://tvhebdo.infinit.net/@@LezT5RYAEehDszTJ/
(Site is all French!)

Prevue Online
http://www.prevue.com/

PRINT ARTICLES

"Chicks Who Kick," *Sacramento Bee,* 27 August 1997.

"La Femme Peta," *Entertainment Weekly* #390, 1 August 1997.

"Nikita Is a USA Hit—She's TV's First Genuine Female Action Hero!" *Montreal Gazette,* 2 August 1997.

"Peta the Great," *Maxim Magazine,* January/February 1998.

"Roy Dupuis' Montreal," *American Way,* 15 February 1998.

Brockway, Laurie Sue, "La Femme Nikita's Roy Dupuis: The Cure for the Common Man," *Single Living Magazine,* September/October 1997.

Cook, John, "New Assignments for Wilson on USA," *San Francisco Sunfay Examiner and Chronicle,* 22 June 1997.

Endrsy, James, "Nikita Pushes Peta Wilson Up the Ladder of Fame," *Florida Today,* 17 August 1997.

Graham, Jefferson, "'Nikita' Star Shoots Straight for the Top: Peta Wilson Knocks 'Em Dead on Cable," *USA TODAY,* 14 April 1997.

Green, Michelle Erica, "La Femme Nikita on Strength, Stamina, and Role Model," *Mania Magazine,* May 1998.

Gross, Edward, "Lady Killer," *Cinescape,* May/June 1997.

Harris, Lyle V., "Channel Surfer: 'La Femme' Resuscitates Female Sleuth Archetype," *The Atlanta Journal and Consitution,* 10 February 1997.

Kelleher, Terry, "Nikita: All Style, No Substance," *Newsday,* 12 January 1997.

King, Susan, "Nikita Knocks Them Dead," *The Philadelphia Inquirer,* August 1997.

King, Susan, "Oui, Nikita," *Los Angeles Times,* 3 August 1997.

King, Susan, "To Her Fans, Nothing Could Be Neater than 'Nikita,'" *Los Angeles Times,* July 1997.

Lang, Steven and Natasha Stoynoff, "On the Move: Femme Fatale Ex-Basketball Star Peta Wilson Kills Them Softly As TV's La Femme Nikita," *People,* 14 April 1997.

Littlefield, Kinney, "'Nikita' Take Her Female Power the Manly Way," *Orange Country Register,* 17 August 1997.

Malcom, Shawna, La Femme Nikita—Ladykiller, *Entertainment Weekly,* 9 January 1998.

McConville, Jim, "'Nikita' Becoming a Real Killer for USA Network," *Electronic Media,* 9, June 1997.

McDonald, Stef, "Peta's Principles," *TV Guide,* 9 June 1997.

Morton, Neil, "In Praise of Alberta Watson," *Elm Street Magazine,* May 1998.

Rubin, Sylvia, "The New Femme Fatale: USA's Popular 'Nikita' an Assasin With Sizzle," *San Francisco Chronicle,* 17 September 1997.

Saunders, Dusty, "Nikita Wins Viewers and Battles with Style," *The Gazette,* 29 August 1997.

Scapperotti, Dan, "La Femme Nikita," *Femme Fatales* 6, no. 2 (1997).

Young, Mark Lerein, "One on One With Nikita," *TV Week,* 23 May 1998.

INDEX

INDEX

Xena Rules!

Whether you've watched her since her early dia-bolical appearances on *Hercules: The Legendary Journeys* or are a newcomer to this syndicated phenomenon, you know *Xena: The Warrior Princess* is the hottest thing on television. But how much do you really know about the show's sizzling star, Lucy Lawless? How similar is she to the sword-swinging, campy heroin she portrays? Everything you've ever wanted to know about both Lucy and Xena is here for the taking, including:

- Biographies of leading characters
- A behind-the-scenes look at the origins and production of the show
- A complete episode guide of the first two seasons
- An encyclopedia of the Xenaverse
- And much, much more!

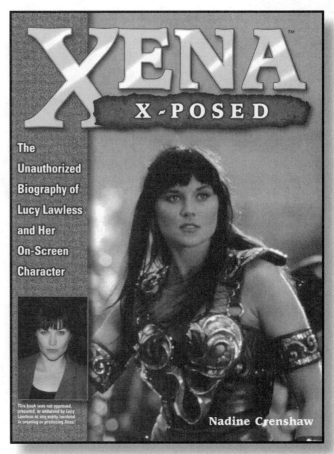

XENA™
X-POSED

The Unauthorized Biography of Lucy Lawless and Her On-Screen Character

This book was not approved, prepared, or endorsed by Lucy Lawless or any entity involved in creating or producing Xena.™

Nadine Crenshaw

ISBN 0-7615-1265-9 / paperback / 256 pages
U.S. $16.95 / Can. $25.00

PRIMA

To order, call (800) 632-8676 or visit us online at www.primapublishing.com

Your Road Map to the Legendary Journeys

Everyone knows Hercules is the toughest of the tough, but how well do you really know the star of *The Legendary Journeys*? You love this weekly dose of eye-candy, but do you know how it all began? The answers are all here. For the first time ever, get a behind-the-scenes look at how a handful of made-for-TV movies became a runaway syndicated phenomenon. This thrilling exposé gives you all the information you desire, including:

- **Biographies of leading characters**
- **Interviews with the show's creators**
- **A complete episode guide of the first three seasons**
- **An A–Z directory featuring every character**
- **And much, much more!**

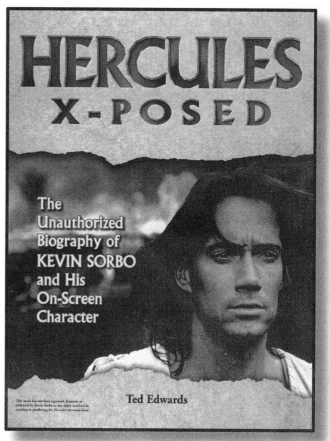

ISBN 0-7615-1366-3 / paperback / 208 pages
U.S. $16.00 / Can. $21.95

To Order Books

Please send me the following items:

Quantity	Title	Unit Price	Total
_____	**Scully X-Posed**	$ **16.00**	$ _____
_____	**Xena X-Posed**	$ **16.95**	$ _____
_____	**Hercules X-Posed**	$ **16.00**	$ _____
_____	**Unauthorized Guide to the X-Files**	$ **16.00**	$ _____
_____	_____	$ _____	$ _____

Subtotal	$ _____
Deduct 10% when ordering 3–5 books	$ _____
7.25% Sales Tax (CA only)	$ _____
8.25% Sales Tax (TN only)	$ _____
5% Sales Tax (MD and IN only)	$ _____
7% G.S.T. Tax (Canada only)	$ _____
Shipping and Handling*	$ _____
Total Order	$ _____

*Shipping and Handling depend on Subtotal.

Subtotal	Shipping/Handling
$0.00–$14.99	$3.00
$15.00–$29.99	$4.00
$30.00–$49.99	$6.00
$50.00–$99.99	$10.00
$100.00–$199.99	$13.50
$200.00+	Call for Quote

Foreign and all Priority Request orders:
Call Order Entry department
for price quote at 916-632-4400
This chart represents the total retail price of books only
(before applicable discounts are taken).

By Telephone: With MC, Visa, or American Express, call 800-632-8676 or 916-632-4400.
Mon–Fri, 8:30–4:30.
WWW: http://www.primapublishing.com

By Internet E-mail: sales@primapub.com
By Mail: Just fill out the information below and send with your remittance to:

Prima Publishing
P.O. Box 1260BK
Rocklin, CA 95677

Name_____

Address_____

City_____ State_____ ZIP_____

MC/Visa/American Express#_____ Exp._____

Check/money order enclosed for $ _____ Payable to Prima Publishing

Daytime telephone _____

Signature _____